H

From the moment she met Dr Rob Martin, pupil midwife Joanna had been determined to see the worst in him. But as their work on the maternity ward of a large Cape Town hospital brought them closer with shared tragedy and happiness it seemed that she just might have been wrong about the doctor—and her own feelings.

Books you will enjoy
in our Doctor Nurse series

HEART OF A NURSE

BY

ELISABETH SCOTT

MILLS & BOON LIMITED
15–16 BROOK'S MEWS
LONDON W1A 1DR

First published in Great Britain 1985
by Mills & Boon Limited

© Elisabeth Scott 1985

Australian copyright 1985
Philippine copyright 1985

ISBN 0 263 75212 7

Set in 10½ on 12 pt Linotron Times
03–1085–48,800

Photoset by Rowland Phototypesetting Limited
Bury St Edmunds, Suffolk
Made and printed in Great Britain by
Richard Clay (The Chaucer Press) Limited
Bungay, Suffolk

CHAPTER ONE

IF I were Mrs Anna in *The King and I*, Joanna thought, I'd whistle a happy tune.

Not that she was afraid, she told herself hastily. Just mildly apprehensive. After all, you can't exactly be afraid of new babies. Or can you?

She peered into the driving mirror of her elderly little car, to check as much as she could of her uniform, and reminded herself that she was a qualified, fully-trained nurse—at least she hoped she would be, when the exam results came out—and of course she could cope with this six months' midwifery course. She'd been lucky to be given the chance to do it, because not all the girls who had done their general with her had been offered the chance of the six months' integrated course. But Joanna knew, without false modesty, that she was a good nurse—her marks at nursing college had always been among the top, and her ward reports unfailingly good.

The maternity hospital wasn't unfamiliar to her, for she had done two months here in her final year, once she had been accepted for this integrated course. Her own training hospital was on the Sea Point side of Cape Town, and she had enjoyed her years there, with the sea to look at from the hospital windows.

Now she would spend her time between the maternity hospital itself, and the huge sprawling hospital farther up the slopes of Table Mountain, the hospital whose name was now world-famous. But babies, Joanna told herself, going up the steps, are just as important as heart transplants. Maybe more.

Smiling at her own thoughts, she didn't see the tall, white-coated figure hurrying out as she hurried in—at least, she didn't see him until she had collided with him.

'Hey, steady on! It's the patients who are in a hurry here, not the nurses!'

He was tall and fair, and his dark blue eyes were extremely amused. And he didn't, Joanna thought furiously, need both arms to keep her from falling!

Typical houseman, she told herself. Almost at the end of his training, and thinks he's God's gift to nurses. Well, as it happens, I don't need arrogant final-year medics in my life.

'Thank you,' she said, as coolly as possible, hoping her deliberate omission of the 'Doctor' wouldn't escape him. 'This nurse, as it happens, is in a hurry.' And then, very sweetly, 'You're probably hurrying off to a lecture, though—sorry if I've held you up.'

Afterwards, she was to remember that instead of being crushed by this, he had laughed, a shout of laughter that had caused a window above their heads to open and a white-capped head to look out.

'Thanks for reminding me, Nurse.' If possible, the blue eyes were more amused than ever. 'I am on my way to a lecture—be seeing you!'

I doubt it, friend, Joanna told him silently as he hurried off down the steps. I've met too many like you through the years.

She tightened her hold on her textbooks and her

notes, and went inside. The other student midwives were gathered there, and when the group was complete, they were greeted by Sister Bennett.

'You know how we work,' she reminded them crisply. 'You've all had some experience here during the last year, on the wards, but before you do any ward work in this course, you will have an intensive fortnight in college. And I do mean intensive. So much so that we start right away—follow me to the lecture theatre, please, and remember, everything you learn, every word of theory, will all too soon have a very practical application.'

Joanna exchanged a few quick words of greeting with some of the other newly-qualified nurses who had been with her at college for General, then she slipped into a seat beside a girl she had met when they did clinic work together a few months ago.

'Hi,' she whispered. 'Glad to see you, Pat. Remind me to tell you about Tracy when we go for tea. What are we having today? "Diseases Associated with Pregnancy." Who's doing that?'

'Dr Martin,' Pat Reed told her. 'One of the registrars. Wait till you see him, he's an absolute honey. Here he is. Don't you think he's terrific?'

He was tall and fair and there was still amusement in his blue eyes. Even from one side of the lecture theatre to the other, Joanna could see that. Not a houseman, she thought, with a sinking feeling—a registrar. And not only that, but one of our lecturers.

And a good lecturer, at that, she had to admit, an hour later, when Dr Martin had finished a clear and concise description of the effect of diabetes on childbearing. With the rest of the class, she filed down the steps to collect the notes he was handing out. Perhaps, she thought, he won't even notice me.

But he did. She saw him glance at her as he handed the notes to Pat, in front of her.

'Here you are, Nurse—Winter.' A glance at her name tag, and then, as he handed her the notes, he leaned towards her. 'You were right—I was hurrying off to a lecture.'

Joanna had always prided herself on her self-possession, but suddenly it deserted her, and she felt a wave of warm colour flood her cheeks.

'Thank you, Doctor,' she said stiffly, furious with herself, and even more furious with this tall, good-looking doctor with the laughter in his eyes and the warm teasing in his voice.

Her friend Pat was waiting for her at the door.

'What did he say to you?' she asked breathlessly.

Joanna hated having to admit to her mistake, but if she didn't say anything, she could see that Pat wouldn't let it go. So, in an extremely offhand voice, she said that she had bumped into him at the door, and had thought he was a houseman.

'He's young to be a registrar,' she said defensively. 'And he—he acts more like a houseman. You know the kind—they expect every nurse to fall at their feet.'

'I believe he's brilliant,' Pat replied, her voice hushed. 'And so good-looking!'

'Not my type at all,' said Joanna with certainty, stirring her sugarless tea with great absorption.

'Oh, how is Colin?' Pat asked. 'He must be almost finished his year in the States.'

'Yes, he is,' Joanna replied. 'He did say, in his last letter, that he might take a few weeks to look around when his job finishes, but that depends on what he's offered here. He's been doing a fair bit of research in the neurological line, and of course that's what he'd like to get into back there.'

'And then?' her friend asked with interest. 'When he gets back, I mean? Will you be getting married?'

'We're not actually engaged,' Joanna said quickly. 'At least, not officially. It didn't make sense, with Colin going off to America and me with my finals, and then this midwifery lot. But—well, of course we have talked about it.'

'He's nice, your Colin,' commented Pat, as they finished their tea and carried the cups back.

Yes, he is, Joanna thought with warm affection. She and Colin had met when she was in her second year, and although at first they had both been part of the crowd, gradually they had become a twosome, and somehow, by the time Colin qualified, and went off to do research in America for a year, they were talking of becoming engaged when he came back.

That night, in the flat she shared with two other nurses, a few streets from the hospital, she finished the letter she had been writing to Colin by telling him about her first day.

'So much to learn,' she wrote. 'And as Sister said, every bit of theory will all too soon have a practical application.' She hesitated, then added a sentence to tell him that their first lecturer had been Dr Robert Martin. 'I don't suppose you'll know him, he's probably a few years older than you are. A good lecturer, but too sure of himself.'

And that, she thought more than once in the next

few days, just about summed up Dr Robert Martin—
Rob, he was apparently called.

'It suits him—has a nice masculine sort of sound,'
Pat said dreamily.

'Well, of course it does,' Joanna agreed briskly. 'He
probably thinks Robert sounds too stuffy. Really,
Pat, it's nurses like you who make doctors like him
what they are!'

Pat's eyes were wide.

'You must admit he's a good lecturer,' she said
reproachfully. 'I don't think I'll ever forget the midwife's responsibility in megaloblastic anaemia of
pregnancy, will you?'

'Probably not,' Joanna allowed. 'But you can read
it all up in your Maggie Myles, you know.'

'I know we can,' Pat agreed. 'But I'd rather hear it
in our Rob's brown velvet voice.'

Joanna shook her head at that, and gave up. Brown
velvet, indeed! Just a voice—quite a pleasant one,
but—brown velvet!

Even during that first college time, she could see
that working here was going to be quite different from
any other sort of hospital. Qualified midwives she
had known had told her this. The patients are
different, the doctors are different, they had said. The
atmosphere is different.

Well, of course, Joanna had always replied briskly.
The patients are all women, for starters, and with all
these babies around, of course the atmosphere is
going to be different. Noisier, for one thing.

But it wasn't really as tangible as any of these
things, she found. Perhaps part of it was that in
general, the people in a maternity hospital were

neither ill nor unhappy, they were there for a specific purpose and for a limited time, and mostly they were actually enjoying being there. Going with Sister into one of the wards for a Baby to Breast demonstration, was almost, Joanna thought, like dropping in on a group of friends spending a morning together. Within a few days, it seemed, the young mothers had become firm friends, sharing confidences, interested in each other's babies, making plans to keep in touch after they all went home.

'Oh yes, that happens,' one of her flatmates, Lynn, who had already done midwifery, agreed. 'They share so much in that short time, I suppose they feel it's a bond that will stand up to a lot. When I was there, we had two women in having their second babies. They'd met when they had their first ones, and actually planned to have their second babies at the same time.'

'Quite some planning,' commented Joanna, impressed.

'Well, it wasn't quite the same day, actually one was almost ready to go home when the other came in,' Lynn admitted. 'I'm glad you do feel that there's something special there, though—I guess I'm pretty hardboiled, but even I get a funny feeling when I give a mother her newly-born baby. And as for the first one you deliver—that's something you won't forget, ever. Mind, remember you've got to fight it out with the housemen for deliveries, they have their quota too.'

Cathy, their third flatmate, looked up from the textbook she was studying.

'I hope I'm accepted for the integrated course

too,' she said softly. 'I'd love working with the babies.'

'You would at first,' Lynn agreed, 'but believe me, a nursery full of squalling babies, and only two of you to deal with them, is the best method of family planning I've ever known! All your broody feelings go right out the window.'

It was no exaggeration, Joanna thought often during that first fortnight of college, to say that this was pretty intensive. The days flew by, filled with lectures, notes, demonstrations, and the evenings were needed for studying. So when she came home after her last college day, to find a note from Lynn saying they'd been invited to a party, she couldn't work up much enthusiasm.

'You go on your own,' she said, when Lynn came off duty just after seven. 'I have plans for this evening.

'I know your plans,' her friend returned. 'Chinese takeaway, feet up, a good read of Maggie Myles.'

'Maggie Myles makes interesting reading,' Joanna protested, defending the student midwives' Bible. 'And actually, you're not entirely right. I was going to write a long letter to Colin, because I don't know how much like writing I'll feel next week, when I'm on the wards.'

'Colin can wait,' Lynn told her. 'Besides, it's time you got to know some more of the people you're working with. Not that everyone will be from the hospital, of course,' she added hastily. 'Kay Evans from Theatre knows lots of people in advertising, and they're always fun.'

'Cathy can go,' suggested Joanna.

'No, thanks,' Cathy said quickly. 'You know I don't like that sort of thing—too many people, too much noise.'

For a moment Joanna's eyes met Lynn's. They both worried about the younger girl, quiet and shy and unwilling to meet people. With them, and with people she knew, she could relax and be herself, but it took her an age, Joanna and Lynn sometimes thought, to get to that stage.

'It isn't really Cathy's thing,' Lynn admitted. 'Come on, Joanna, we won't stay late, I'm on at seven tomorrow morning.'

Suddenly light dawn on Joanna, and she laughed.

'And your car's broken down,' she said. 'It's a lift you need, not really my company!'

'Well, that too,' admitted Lynn unrepentantly and cheerfully. 'But you'll enjoy it.'

Joanna gave in then, and the usual scramble to get ready to go out began, with Cathy on the sidelines ready to lend a scarf, sandals, earrings, to bring coffee and a sandwich to Joanna in the bath, and Lynn in her room.

'Have a nice time,' she called as they left. 'Got your keys?'

'Younger than either of us, but she fusses like an old mother hen,' Joanna commented affectionately as they got into the car. 'Maybe if we had just a few people around, Lynn, before she gets too heavily into studying again—you know, a sort of quietish evening. Something to drink, a few snacks, not too many people. I think we should.'

'We could,' Lynn agreed, without much enthusiasm. 'Sounds a bit dull for my tastes.'

'It's not for your tastes or mine,' Joanna reminded her. 'Anyway, let's think about it.'

The party they were going to was in a big old house in Observatory, not far from the big hospital. Because they were late, parking was hard to find in the narrow little streets, and Joanna had to drive up and down a few times before she found a space for her car, and once again she was grateful that it was so small.

The door was open, and the wide and shaded stoep, or verandah, was filled with people. So, Joanna thought soon, was every room in the house. One large room had been cleared for dancing, and another, with cushions and rugs around the walls, seemed to be the twosome room. Joanna stepped over assorted legs and feet and made her way into a third, smaller room, where she thought she had caught a glimpse of some plates of food. Sausage rolls, she thought with satisfaction, and with luck, from the bakery on the main road. She took a bite, and decided she had been right.

'Hungry as well as in a hurry,' a voice beside her commented lazily.

Joanna choked on her second bit of sausage roll, and a large hand patted her back.

'Look up at the roof,' Rob Martin advised her kindly. 'That's my mother's advice for anyone choking, and it does seem to work.'

Strangely enough, it did. Gradually Joanna recovered. But why, she thought between embarrassment and annoyance, did this man always have to see her at a disadvantage?

'Thank you,' she said coolly. 'I'm all right now.'

The deep blue eyes studied her, from the tip of the white sandals she had borrowed from Cathy, to her hair, pinned up on top of her head but not securely enough, she realised under his scrutiny, for a few strands were already escaping.

'Yes, you're certainly all right now,' Rob Martin agreed. He took her hand. 'Let's dance.'

Until he had materialised beside her, Joanna had found her feet already itching to dance. Now, perversely, she decided she didn't want to.

'I don't want to dance at the moment,' she said, hoping she sounded her usual composed self again. Because I cannot bear, she told herself fiercely, these doctors who think every nurse is just waiting to fall into their arms!

'All right, then, we'll talk,' Rob Martin returned pleasantly, and somehow she found herself being led out of the house and into the garden. 'I know where there's a garden seat,' he told her.

I'll just bet you do, Joanna thought inelegantly. And I'll bet you know it pretty well.

'Right,' he said, sitting her down on the garden bench and sitting beside her, with one arm along the back of the seat. 'You have the advantage of me—I only know you're Nurse Winter. Tell me more about yourself.'

His voice is like brown velvet, she thought, and instantly was furious with herself.

'Right,' she said sweetly. 'What do you want to know—other than that my name is Joanna, and I'm engaged to a doctor who is doing research in the States at the moment?'

Unofficially engaged, she added silently, but you don't need to know that, Dr Rob Martin.

'I wondered why you were here on your own,' the

man beside her said, and although she didn't look at him, she could hear the smile in his voice. 'Doesn't he mind?'

'Not at all,' Joanna told him truthfully, for she and Colin had talked about this before he left, and agreed that neither of them would live monastic lives.

'Broadminded fellow,' Rob Martin observed. 'Then he probably wouldn't mind this either.'

She had already put him down as a pretty fast and smooth worker, but she hadn't expected him to be this fast. Or this smooth, she found herself thinking in confusion, as his lips found hers and his arms drew her closer to him. And then she wasn't thinking at all. Until suddenly she came to her senses, and pulled free.

'Remember,' she said breathlessly—and who wouldn't be breathless, she defended herself, after a kiss like that?—'I'm engaged.'

His lips were still very close to hers.

'Did you remember?' he asked her, his voice warm and teasing.

And Joanna, dismayed, had to admit to herself that she had thought of nothing and no one but Dr Rob Martin, when she was in his arms.

CHAPTER TWO

'CHEMISTRY,' Joanna said loudly, fighting the drowsy contentment of a girl who has just been well and truly kissed. 'Chemistry, that's all.' And she lifted her chin and glared at the tall fair man beside her.

Rob Martin said nothing, but there was laughter in his eyes.

'In any case,' she added, less loudly, and with a determined smile, 'what's in a kiss?'

'Exactly,' he agreed. 'Just what I was asking myself. What is in a kiss, indeed?' He moved towards her purposefully. 'Should we try a little more chemistry, Joanna, and perhaps we can find out?'

'No, we won't,' Joanna replied hastily. 'I wouldn't mind a glass of wine, though.'

'Dry, I should think,' said Rob Martin, with an assurance that made her look at him suspiciously. He raised his eyebrows. 'You look like the kind of girl who likes her wine dry and white and well chilled.'

Just what is that supposed to mean? Joanna asked herself when he had left her. And then, mentally, she shrugged her shoulders. Nothing, except that Dr Robert Martin has had plenty of experience in both girls and wine, I guess.

She was annoyed and more than a little taken aback by her own reaction to the warmth of his lips on hers. It wasn't the first time, in the year that Colin had been away, that she had been kissed. The other kisses had been—pleasant, right at the time, warm and friendly. But Rob Martin's kiss—Chemistry, Joanna reminded herself again. Just chemistry. He isn't even the kind of man I go for. Too good-looking by far, and too sure of himself by far. Knows the kind of wine I like, indeed!

She wasn't sure, afterwards, whether it was annoyance or cowardice, but suddenly she knew that she didn't want to be here when Rob Martin came back with a glass of chilled dry white wine and sat down in the dark summer garden. Quickly she stood up and hurried into the house, through to where there were plenty of people, plenty of noise, and dancing.

She was claimed by a friend of Colin's right away, and it was only much later, across the room, that she saw Rob Martin dancing with a blonde girl. A good dancer, too, she admitted to herself, knowing that she would have been surprised if he hadn't been.

He raised his hand casually to her, and Joanna, just as casually, raised hers in reply, before she turned away and went on dancing with even more enthusiasm.

'I don't want to be a spoilsport,' said Lynn, later, beside her, 'But you weren't all that keen on coming, and I do have to get up early, but I could find someone to give me a lift if you want to stay.'

Joanna shook her head.

'No, I'm happy to come now,' she replied. 'Where's Cheryl?'

Together they found the girl who had invited them to the party, and thanked her, then made their way out of the house and down the garden path. No sign of our handsome doctor, Joanna thought, he's probably got the little blonde on the garden seat now.

'Problems,' Lynn said tersely as they reached Joanna's small car. It had been well and truly parked in, and Joanna, dismayed, didn't see how she was to get out.

'I'll get in, and you can guide me,' she said without too much hope, and began manoeuvring the small car. But five minutes later the car seemed, if anything, to be in a worse position. Suddenly the long, busy day, and the party after it, and now this frustration, were all too much for Joanna. She put her head down on her arms.

'Are you crying?' Rob Martin's voice asked with interest.

Heavens, Joanna thought, I'm being haunted by the man! She lifted her head and looked at him. He was standing beside Lynn, and the small blonde girl was beside him, and Rob's arm was around her shoulders casually. Casually, Joanna thought, and possessively.

'No,' she said clearly, 'I'm not crying, I'm swearing.'

'Let me try,' he suggested.

She shrugged.

'You won't be able to do anything,' she told him with certainty.

Five minutes later the small yellow car was safely out in the narrow street, with not a mark on the cars behind and in front of it, and Joanna was thanking Rob Martin, somewhat stiffly.

'Not at all,' the big fair doctor replied cheerfully. 'Glad to be of some help.' He patted the car's snub bonnet. 'I used to have a beetle myself, maybe it recognised that. 'Bye, girls. You on duty tomorrow,

Lynn? I might see you, if my eclamptic lady has to be hurried on. Don't worry about the wine, Joanna.'

'What did he mean by that?' Lynn asked curiously, as they got into the car.

'He had some wine for me, but we—didn't find each other again,' Joanna explained vaguely, watching as Rob Martin opened the passenger door of a sleek grey sports car and helped the blonde girl in. 'I didn't know you knew him, Lynn.'

'Knew him? Everyone knows our Rob,' Lynn told her. She shook her head. 'He and I had quite a thing going at one time, but it didn't last long—that's the way it is with Rob. Funny, he's one of the few men I know—actually, right now I can't think of any other— you can be madly in love with for a while, and then it's over, but you're still friends. Really friends.'

Joanna watched the grey car pull away.

'He must have a fair number of friends,' she observed.

'Oh, he does,' Lynn agreed. 'Everyone knows what he's like. He never makes any promises, so you go into it with your eyes open, you know you'll have a ball for a short time, and that's it, he moves on to the next.'

Joanna drove along the quiet midnight street and turned into the parking area for their own flat.

'All very well now,' she commented, 'when he's young enough to get away with it. But he can't go on with the Peter Pan act for the rest of his life.'

'He's just waiting for the right girl,' her friend said sleepily, putting her feet back into her shoes. 'How am I ever going to be on duty for seven tomorrow?'

'I've no idea,' Joanna replied, without too much

sympathy. 'See you when you come home. Are you on a one-four?'

They were in the lift now, and Lynn nodded.

'I can sleep for a bit then, before I face being on again from four till seven,' she said, and smothered a yawn. 'Is Cathy off tomorrow? Oh, of course, she's at college, I'd forgotten, so she'll be at home. Are you two doing the shopping? I'll be home just after one, so keep me something for lunch, will you?'

Nice having a Saturday off, Joanna told herself the next day, getting up when she felt like it, having a leisurely breakfast after her bath, and then going to the supermarket with Cathy to do the grocery shopping.

'We'd better make the most of this,' she said to the younger girl. 'Let's have a coffee before we go back and offload this lot. I'm working next Saturday, for sure, and you only have another week of this college block, so you'll be back to the usual unsociable hours too.'

'I don't mind,' said Cathy, as they took their coffees to a small table.

'Actually, I don't mind too much either,' Joanna admitted. 'I think it's nice having a day off in the middle of the week—nice for shopping, or for the beach. But we all complain, every nurse does, as a matter of course. Just as we complain about night duty—although, come to think of it, that really does need complaining about. I'm barely human when I'm on night duty.'

Cathy smiled, and Joanna thought, not for the first time, how very pretty she was when didn't look so shy and serious.

'I know that,' she returned. 'You were on night duty when I moved in with you and Lynn—I was terrified of you!' She stirred her coffee. 'Night duty at a maternity hospital should be more interesting, though—surely there should be more happening?'

'Could be,' said Joanna. 'I just don't function well on upside-down hours!'

The pleasant Saturday morning was completed and rounded off by finding a letter from Colin waiting in the letter-box. Joanna saved it until she and Cathy had put away all the shopping, then she lay down on her bed to read it.

Colin's letters were always amusing, he could always find something funny to tell her, and she smiled now as she read about his weekend visit to the home of a colleague on the research staff, and the interest and attentions of the two teenage girls who lived next door. But yet, when she had finished and had laid down the last sheet and looked once again at his hastily-scrawled—Got to go now, all my love, Colin—she found herself looking at his photograph, then back to the letter, and somehow finding that even the two together didn't add up to the Colin she knew and loved. He—wasn't real, right now, she found herself thinking.

'Cup of tea, Joanna?' asked Cathy at the door. 'Nice letter?'

'Yes—Colin always writes a good letter,' Joanna said quickly—too quickly, she thought as she said it. 'Thanks for the tea, Cathy. Listen to this bit.'

She read out Colin's description of the young American girls trying to copy his accent.

'It's not even genuine South African,' Joanna told

Cathy. 'His parents are Scottish, and there's a hint of that as well.'

'He looks nice, your Colin,' Cathy said softly.

'He is nice—very nice,' Joanna replied soberly, ashamed of the strange thoughts she had been having.

From the wall, Colin's hazel eyes looked down at the two girls.

'He looks,' Cathy said thoughtfully, 'as if he's just going to smile. A quiet sort of smile—sort of as if he's laughing at himself, as well as at other things.'

Joanna looked at her young friend, a little taken aback, because this was very true.

'You'll like him,' she said, knowing this would also be true. 'Actually most people do like Colin, from old ladies and babies through everyone else on the way.'

'Dogs, too?' asked Cathy, smiling, for Joanna always maintained that dogs were better judges of character than people were.

'Dogs, too,' Joanna agreed, and now the strange and distant feeling was gone, and once again Colin was Colin, the man she loved, the man she was going to marry, some time.

Joanna had forgotten, in the months between the last time she had worked here, and now, just how tiny new babies were. When she had started on the ward, working with mothers and with babies, she was grateful that at first all she had to do with the babies was to take them to their mothers for feeding, and then back to the nursery afterwards.

But within a few days, she found to her relief that she felt much more confident, and somehow this got through to the babies.

'They know if you think you're going to drop them,' Lynn told her, handing over a firmly-wrapped bundle. 'You see, already he knows you've found the right way to hold him, and your hands are firm.'

The baby had stopped crying, and although Joanna knew he was too young to be seeing her, his blue eyes did seem to be searching her face.

'Right, take him to his mum,' Lynn said briskly. 'Plenty more ready.'

It was a fairly easy start, Joanna thought in these first few days, being on the post-natal ward. There was plenty to do, and there never seemed to be enough time to fit everything in before the next feeding-time for the babies arrived. But mostly the patients were well, and happy to co-operate in every way, and there were few dramas or crises.

She had been on the ward for a week, and she was, as always, trying to hurry without looking as if she was hurrying, when a loud and insistent buzz sent her from the Duty Room, where she had been working on charts under Sister's supervision, to the ward.

'Nurse, I'm bleeding badly,' the woman in the end bed told her, her eyes wide and anxious. Joanna's eyes took in the extreme pallor of her face and the beads of sweat on her forehead, even as she made a swift examination, and confirmed that she was haemorrhaging. Afterwards, she remembered that Sister had been right when she told them that everything they learned in theory would all too soon have a practical application. Without any need to wonder what to do, she took pads from the locker, applied pressure, and at the same time called to one of the other nurses, remembering, too, to keep her voice calm.

'It's all right, Mrs Terry, the doctor will be here soon,' she reassured the shocked woman.

Within a few minutes Sister was there, and Rob Martin with her.

'Good, Nurse Winter,' said Sister, checking what Joanna had done, swiftly, professionally.

Joanna stood back then, waiting until she should be needed, and admiring, with a little reluctance, Rob Martin's sure and skilful ability. Together he and Sister set up a drip, and he gave the woman an injection to counter the shock she was in, then, without more than one brief glance in Joanna's direction, he was off, striding down the ward, giving Sister instructions to call him if he was needed.

'A very competent young man, our Dr Martin,' Sister observed when she came back.

So he should be, Joanna thought, in his position. And she said nothing, determined that she wasn't going to join the Rob Martin Fan Club. After all, he was a registrar, obviously working towards a consultancy, of course he should be good.

And more than once in the next few days she had occasion to have Sister's opinion confirmed. Rob Martin was indeed a very competent young man.

And knows it, she thought sometimes, but even as she thought it, she knew that she wasn't really being fair, for there was nothing in Rob Martin's manner as a doctor that really justified this.

As a man, of course, he's certainly too sure of himself, she reminded herself from time to time—and reminded herself, too, that this was why she felt this undoubted antagonism towards him. And from time to time the wayward memory would return of his lips warm and demanding on hers—and of her own immediate response to him.

Chemistry, she told herself. You don't need to like a man to—er—to respond when he kisses you.

The small side wards were usually used by private patients, but in Joanna's third week, Sister moved one of the patients from the general ward into a room on her own.

'Fortunately,' she told her staff, 'we're not too full at the moment, and in the circumstances, it's better for Carol Harding to be in on her own. She's only here for another two days, then she'll be going.'

'And the baby will be adopted?' Joanna asked quietly.

'Yes, Nurse Winter, the baby will be adopted. She's been very sensible about the whole thing, knows it's the best thing for the baby. I think she's looking forward to taking up her life again, and just as well, too.'

Lynn turned to Joanna as they went out of the room together.

'If you ask me,' she said, 'this young Carol is quite a hard case. Said to me yesterday that she can't wait to go dancing again, and look at all the sunbathing she's missed.'

I'm not so sure, Joanna thought, for sometimes she had caught a glimpse of something in Carol Harding's eyes that made her wonder if she was indeed as hard as she pretended to be.

Two days later, when the girl was getting ready to

be collected to go home, Joanna went to her room in answer to the bell.

'Almost ready, Carol?' she asked.

Carol nodded.

'My uncle's collecting me in half an hour,' she said brightly, 'and putting me on the Jo'burg plane.' She smiled. 'My mum's told all the neighbours I didn't like it here in Cape Town, wanted to get back where the action is.' She shrugged. 'She could have told them the truth, for all I care, but that's the way she wants it. Hey, I just thought—maybe I'd better have a last look at it—the baby, I mean. Is that OK?'

'Yes, I'm sure that will be all right,' Joanna replied carefully. 'I'll just check with Sister.'

Sister Bennett, preoccupied with a jaundiced baby, only nodded when Joanna asked if she could take Carol's baby to her, so Joanna lifted the tiny scrap from her cot.

'She's a pretty baby, Carol,' she said, as she handed the baby to the girl.

'Not bad,' Carol agreed, her voice offhand. 'I'm glad she looks a bit like me—I'll have some idea what she'll look like when I see old photos of me when I was a kid.'

Next door, in the Duty Room, the telephone rang.

'I'll have to answer that,' said Joanna. 'The others are at tea. I'll be back in a minute for her.'

A few moments later she put the telephone down and turned to go back into the small private room. But at the door she stopped.

Carol's head was bent over her baby, and her long fair hair fell over her face. But Joanna could see that there were tears running down her cheeks.

'Now you be a good girl,' she was saying, and there was a warmth and a softeness in her voice that Joanna hadn't heard before. 'You're going to go and live with some people who can give you a real family life, and maybe later on you'll have a brother or a sister. You'll be happy, my baby, I know you'll be happy. I just wish I could—'

Her voice broke then, and she buried her face in the baby's blanket.

I don't know what to do, and I don't know what to say, Joanna thought, shaken. And I've got to say something.

Carol hadn't seen her, and she backed out of the room and went into the Duty Room. There was no one else around, and she sat down at the desk, and now there were tears in her own eyes. This is no use, she told herself. How can you help that poor girl when you're letting yourself get so upset?

'Nurse, can I have—'

She turned round, to see Rob Martin standing in the door, a patient's chart in his hand. Quickly she brushed the back of her hand across her eyes, but he had seen.

'Joanna, what's wrong, girl?' he asked her, and the warmth and the sympathy in his voice were so unexpected that Joanna, to her own surprise when she thought about it later, found herself telling him just why she was so upset.

CHAPTER THREE

IT was surprisingly easy to talk to Rob Martin, to tell him how all the time she had been here in the hospital, the teenage mother had behaved as if the whole business of having a baby and giving it up for adoption was just a nuisance, and the sooner it was over the better.

'But now, when I heard her voice, when I saw the way she was holding the baby—she loves her little girl, and it hurts her to part with her, and I feel so inadequate, because I want to help her, and I don't know how to,' Joanna finished shakily.

Rob, sitting on the edge of the desk, leaned across and dried her eyes with a tissue.

'That's the first thing,' he said, and now, as well as warm sympathy, there was a practical, businesslike note in his voice, and this helped Joanna more than anything. 'Do your crying later, Joanna—you will. Young Carol isn't the first, nor the last by a long way, that you'll have to help through moments like this. You've been pitchforked into this one a little early, but maybe that isn't a bad thing. And don't be fooled by a hard-as-nails attitude—sure, sometimes that's exactly what it is, but not every time.'

He stood up.

'I could go and talk to her,' he said quietly. 'I've had to do it many times. I know Carol—I delivered her baby. But you've got to do it at some stage, and I think maybe you could help her through this.'

He took both her hands and pulled her to her feet.

'What am I going to say?' Joanna asked him.

'Reinforce her decision to let the baby be adopted,' he said. 'You know, and she knows, that it's the right thing and the best thing. Let her know that you understand that she loves the baby, and let her know that that's a good thing, for her and for the baby. Ask her if she has a name for the baby.'

Joanna looked at him, questioning.

'The baby's only five days old, and she's going to be adopted. After today, Carol won't see her. Why should she have given her a name?'

'Just ask her,' Rob Martin repeated. 'Oh, and Joanna, one more thing. Sister will have spoken to her, but make certain she's coming back to the Birth Control Clinic, so that we don't see her in here again!'

When Joanna went in to the small room next door, Carol had recovered. Her head was high and her voice light and bright as she held the baby out to Joanna.

'Here, better take it back to the nursery,' she said, 'before it starts bawling.'

I could just leave the whole thing, Joanna thought, now that she seems to have got over it. I could just do as she says, take the baby back, and forget the whole thing.

But she knew that she wouldn't be able to do that, with the memory of the softness of this girl's voice as she talked to her baby, of the tears she had shed, alone.

'Carol,' she said gently, 'you really are doing the best thing for her. Somewhere there's a man and a woman who are longing for a baby, and they'll love her, and give her a happy life, and they'll do it more easily than you would be able to on your own.'

The fair hair was tossed back.

'Of course I'm doing the right thing,' Carol replied. 'What in the world would I do with a baby? Believe me, Nurse, I've got plenty of plans to enjoy myself, now that this is over.'

Almost defeated, Joanna took the baby from her. If she refuses to admit it, there's nothing I can do, she thought. And then she remembered what Rob Martin had said.

'What's her name?' she asked, looking at the baby's sleeping face.

All the colour left Carol's face.

'She doesn't have a name,' she said quickly. 'They'll give her a name, the one they choose for her, when she goes to them.'

'I know that,' Joanna agreed, 'but don't you have a name for her yourself? A special name?'

Slowly the brightness and the coolness left Carol's blue eyes.

'I call her Daisy,' she whispered. 'From that book, *Princess Daisy*, see. And she looks sort of like a little flower.'

'Daisy,' Joanna said softly. 'Yes, you're right, it's perfect for her. You know, Carol, you will always be able to think of her as Daisy. For these few days, and for the rest of your life, she'll be Daisy to you. And no one can take that from you.'

Carol wept, then, and Joanna laid the baby gently down on the bed and held the girl in her arms until the tears were over. And then, when Carol had recovered, she reminded her of what Sister had said about coming back for her check-up, and to the Birth Control Clinic.

'I'm going to take her back now,' she said steadily. 'Give her to me, will you, Carol?'

The girl lifted the baby up, her eyes on the tiny sleeping face, and kissed her gently before she handed her to Joanna.

''Bye now, little Daisy,' she whispered.

Joanna, her own throat tight, took the baby back to the nursery, then went back to her charts in the Duty Room. She had almost finished what she was doing when Rob Martin came back along the corridor with Sister, discussing a diabetic patient whose progress wasn't as good as it should have been.

'So as well as the four-hourly temperatures, in case of sepsis, Sister, I'd like her to start on graduated exercises, and I want her ambulant by tomorrow, to minimise the risk of thrombo-embolism.'

'We'll do that, Dr Martin,' Sister replied briskly. 'I feel myself she'll come on better now that she knows the baby is all right—I'm going to the nursery now to give my nurses Dr Abbott's feeding instructions for him.'

Joanna heard Sister's feet tapping briskly down the corridor, then Rob Martin put his head round the door.

'I thought I might find you here,' he said. 'You did a good job on that, Joanna—I couldn't help hearing some of it. She'll be all right now—I've just said goodbye to her, and I'm happier about her.'

'Thank you for your help,' said Joanna, a little awkwardly.

'You know me,' Rob replied cheerfully. 'Proper Sir

Galahad—nothing is too much trouble where a pretty nurse is concerned!'

'Get out of here, I have work to do,' Joanna told him, laughing, and in some way that she preferred not to explore, extremely relieved to find herself dealing with Rob Martin as she expected him to be. For there was something disturbing and much too thought-provoking about the way he had talked to her, about the warm sympathy in his dark blue eyes and in his voice. None of that fitted with the way she had him taped. In a way, she thought, he was much easier to deal with when he was being his usual arrogant self, behaving as if he was the answer to every nurse's prayer.

A few days later she started on Labour Ward, and there was no time for thinking about Dr Rob Martin or anyone else. So much to do, and so much to learn, she found herself thinking, as she hurried around with the other student midwives between deliveries, cleaning the tables and the trolleys and the sterilisers, putting clean soft sheets into the tiny cots ready for the newly-born babies, making sure that any drips that might be necessary were ready, checking the sterile packs, testing the diathermy machine and the emergency lights. To any trained nurse, like Joanna, most of this was routine, but there were the specific instructions and necessities for childbirth.

'A good midwife is essentially a good nurse,' Joanna chanted, handing her well-read copy of Maggie Myles' *Textbook for Midwives* to Cathy, when she came off duty after the first day on Labour Ward. 'Thanks for running my bath, Cathy, you're an angel.'

'Just as well I'm an off-duty angel too, today,' Cathy replied. 'Do you want me to hear the rest?'

Joanna stripped off her uniform and her pants and bra, and stepped into the bath.

'Yes, please, just that first bit.' She soaped herself, then lay back, her aching feet wiggling in the warm water. 'She will endeavour to give comfort, relieve pain, conserve strength, prevent exhaustion, injury and loss of blood. Maintain cleanliness, antisepsis and asepsis throughout labour. Exercise vigilant observation. This is an integral part of good nursing, and the midwife requires—' She stopped. 'What does the midwife require?' she asked Cathy anxiously.

'Sufficient knowledge and experience to enable her to recognise normal progress and detect deviations from the natural course,' Cathy read.

'Thanks, I'll do the next bit later,' said Joanna, taking the towel from the side of the bath. 'Lynn comes off at seven, doesn't she? I know she wants to go out, I'd better get supper ready fast.'

It was her night to cook, but Cathy came through and made a salad while Joanna grilled sausages, and cleaned and cut up some small new potatoes. By the time Lynn came in there was enough hot water again for her to have her bath, and when she came through to the kitchen dressed ready to go out, Joanna was setting sausages and potatoes on their plates, and Cathy had just cut some brown bread.

'No more dates with doctors for me,' Lynn announced halfway through supper. 'Tonight I'm going to a different sort of theatre—that divine Michael I met at the Pig and Whistle is taking me to the Baxter, to see a Tom Stoppard play. He's absolutely oozing Irish charm! When we have this party, girls, I want to invite him.'

'Party?' Joanna and Cathy echoed together, looking at her.

'Well, not really party,' Lynn said hastily. 'Just a—sort of pleasant evening with friends. Remember, Joanna, you and I talked about it.'

Cathy's back was turned while she poured three mugs of coffee, and Lynn jabbed a finger at her unsuspecting back and frowned fiercely at Joanna.

'Remember?' she said again, and Joanna did remember that they had talked vaguely of an evening with not too many people, so that Cathy wouldn't be overwhelmed and retreat into her shell.

'What sort of evening are we thinking about?' she asked with suspicion, because she and Lynn had been flatmates for two years, and she knew well how these quiet evenings could grow and grow.

Lynn opened her eyes wide.

'Just a few people,' she said vaguely. 'My risotto, Cathy's salad, your garlic bread, some wine. Civilised conversation, low music—you know.'

'And your charming Michael, of course, sharing it all,' Joanna suggested.

Lynn smiled. 'Of course,' she agreed. 'I thought maybe fourteen or fifteen people, we can fit in just about that. Cheryl, Tracey, Donald, Johan, Nell, Rob, Beth—'

'Wait a minute,' Joanna put in. 'Rob who?'

'Rob Martin—he's an old buddy of mine, and now that you know him too, I'd like to ask him,' said Lynn. 'Heavens, look at the time! I'll be late.'

'Wait a minute,' Joanna said firmly, catching her

friend by the arm. 'Why Rob Martin? We haven't had him here before.'

'He's been away, only got back a few months ago,' Lynn told her. 'He's great fun, Joanna.'

'He's too sure of himself by half,' Joanna replied. 'I don't like men like that.'

'Come off it, Joanna,' Lynn said mildly. 'You're a big girl, you don't have to do more than say hello and goodbye to him—I like him, and like I say, he's good fun.'

Joanna shrugged, giving in. But how ridiculous, she told herself later, to have become so annoyed, I've always kept my cool, what is it about this man that makes me behave in such a peculiar way?

Determinedly, once again, she put him out of her mind, and returned her attention to learning the next paragraph in her textbook.

More and more, in these first days she was on Labour Ward, she found that what she was learning in theory was very real and very immediate. It was right, she found herself thinking with pleasure one busy afternoon, that no matter how much there was to do, a midwife should take the time to give her patients emotional support, and company, as well as doing whatever was necessary from a medical point of view.

She looked forward, with some apprehension, to her first delivery, but some of the last intake of student midwives, as well as the housemen, desperately needed babies to make up their quota, and the new girls were all content, for the moment, to stand back and observe.

But I think, Joanna told herself one day when she came off duty, if I had to, I could cope now. She changed quickly into shorts and a tee-shirt, slipped her uniform back on over them, and hurried out to her car. Today she had a one-four, which meant that she was off between one and four, and there would be time, she had decided, to have a walk in Newlands Forest before it was time to go back on duty. She drove up past the big hospital, along beyond the University, crossed to the parking place among the trees and slipped her uniform off.

Quiet and peaceful and cool, she thought with satisfaction. And then she saw another car turning into the Forest Reserve.

'Damn!' she said loudly and angrily. And she said it again when the car drove right up and parked beside her own car.

'Great idea, on a day like this,' Dr Rob Martin observed, getting out of his car. 'Which way are we going?'

Joanna was speechless.

'I have a goldfish who looks remarkably like you do right now,' Rob Martin remarked.

She found her voice.

'How did you—what did you—why—?' She took a deep breath. 'What are you doing here?' she asked coolly.

'Coming for a walk with you,' he said, surprised. 'Oh, I see what you mean. I knew you had an after-noon off, and so did I, so I followed you.' He looked at her approvingly. 'I do like a girl who dresses for the occasion. Or should I say undresses?'

Joanna was uncomfortably aware of the briefness of her shorts, not to mention the cool but see-through look of her shirt.

'Right,' Rob said briskly, 'which way are we going? Along by the reservoir? Unfortunately we don't have time to go to Kirstenbosch and back—maybe next time we could leave a car at each end.'

Joanna took a deep breath and a decision. This arrogant young man was not going to spoil her walk, she wouldn't let him.

'I,' she said clearly, 'plan on walking along to the end of the reservoir and back. You're very welcome to come with me if you want to, although as a matter of fact, I come up here to be alone.'

And without waiting for him to reply, she turned and walked up through the forest, putting from her mind the disturbing memory of the way he had helped her to deal with Carol Harding's grieving at parting with her baby. This is the way he really is, she told herself quickly. That was just—being professional.

She was glad that she was accustomed to walking, glad that she could keep up the fairly brisk pace Rob was setting. As always when she was walking in the forest, she had a moment's longing for a dog running ahead of her.

'I always think it's strange to walk here without a dog,' Rob remarked, and she looked at him, unable to keep her surprise from her face.

'I was just thinking the same,' she told him, before she could stop herself.

He took her hand lightly in his.

'Come and walk with me on Camps Bay beach some time,' he suggested, 'and we'll take my Rufus out, and you can share him for walks.'

'Why Camps Bay?' Joanna asked suspiciously.

'I have a cottage there,' he told her, and Joanna,

with good reason, reminded herself that he certainly wasn't the first young doctor who had told her he had a beach cottage.

'Come up and see my sandcastles?' she said.

He shook his head.

'Believe it or not, Joanna, I really did mean just that—come and share my dog for a little.' He looked at his watch. 'Better turn—you're on at four, I suppose.'

They walked back in silence, but once, through a break in the trees, Rob pointed out to her, an arm around her shoulders for a moment, the vista of Cape Town and the sea spread out below them.

When they got back to the cars he opened the boot of his, and produced a flask of coffee. Joanna, impressed in spite of herself, was glad to accept, and they sat down on the carpet of pine needles, with his car rug spread out. When he had finished his coffee, Rob lay back and closed his eyes.

What ridiculously long eyelashes he has for a man, Joanna found herself thinking. She cleared her throat.

'Tired?' she asked him, her voice distant, professional.

'A Caesar and a placenta praevia last night,' he said, his eyes still shut. 'Could be more tonight, too.' Unexpectedly, he opened his eyes, and Joanna looked away quickly, but not quickly enough.

He sat up. 'I've been thinking about that chemistry business,' he said, his voice warm and drowsy. 'It's an interesting thought.'

It seemed ridiculous to act surprised and outraged, so Joanna sat still when he put his arms around her and drew her towards him. Cool and aloof, and a little amused, she told herself. That's the way to deal with him.

Then his lips were on hers, warm and searching, and it happened again, the immediate, unbelievable response of her body to his.

This time it was Rob who drew back, releasing her slowly, with reluctance.

'You're quite a girl, Joanna Winter,' he murmured, and she was taken aback to find that his voice wasn't quite steady. 'Maybe Winter by name, but certainly not by nature—'

Joanna, trying to recover, felt that some explanation was necessary.

'You just—have a peculiar effect on me,' she said, 'that's all.'

He raised his eyebrows. 'All?' he asked softly.

She scrambled to her feet. 'I have to go,' she said quickly. 'I'll be late on duty.'

Without looking back at him, she got into her car and drove off, glad that for once her car had started right away. And glad, later, that she was kept so busy on Labour Ward that there just was no time for her to think about Dr Rob Martin, and the way she felt when he was anywhere near her.

There was a letter from Colin waiting for her when she went home that night, and somehow the familiarity of his handwriting was comforting. She put the kettle on, made herself a cup of tea, and sat down to read her letter.

A few moments later, her tea and everything else forgotten, she read it again, to make sure.

Colin was coming home earlier than he had expected. There was the sudden chance of a job in the Neurology Department here in Cape Town, and his boss had agreed to release him. There was no question, now, of taking any time for a holiday, if he wanted this job he had to be there by the end of the month. He would see her soon, he finished, and he loved her.

Joanna sat with the letter in her hand. For almost a year they had been apart, she and Colin, he had been only a photograph, and letters. As she had been to him. Now he was coming home, in a few weeks they would be together again.

And just for a moment, Joanna wasn't quite sure how she felt about this.

CHAPTER FOUR

'You must be so thrilled, Joanna,' Cathy said when Joanna told her.

'I am,' Joanna replied quickly—too quickly, something inside her questioned, but she silenced the thought. 'Yes, it's wonderful—sooner than we expected. It's going to be lovely having Colin back.'

And of course it will be, she thought with increasing certainty. It was only natural that she should have had a moment's—surprise, adjustment—because a year was a long time for two people to be apart. We had to get used to being away from each other, she remembered; now we'll have to get used to being together again.

'Do you think you'll get engaged as soon as Colin gets back?' asked Lynn, when she came in and heard the news. 'Should we be looking for a new flatmate?'

'Oh no,' Joanna replied hastily. 'I'm sure Colin wouldn't want that, and nor would I. Give us time, Lynn.'

For a moment her friend's eyes held hers.

'You need time?' asked Lynn, with a perception that brought a tide of colour to Joanna's cheeks. She was grateful when Lynn began to talk about the party they were planning, wondering if they should postpone it until Colin arrived.

'I don't think so,' Joanna said quickly, instinctively. 'I don't know exactly when he'll be here, Lynn. No, let's go ahead when we planned it. Remember how difficult it was fitting in all the off-duties?'

And that, she told herself firmly, was quite true, with so many medical people involved. It hadn't been at all easy fixing a time when all the people they wanted to invite would be able to come. No, going ahead with the party before Colin arrived had absolutely nothing to do with a sudden disconcerting picture of Colin and herself together—watched by Rob Martin's dark blue eyes, lazy and amused.

But whatever she thought of him as a man, she had no doubt at all that he was an extremely good doctor, and beyond that, an exceptionally lucid lecturer. Joanna found that the lectures he gave to the student nurses were among the best in their course. Now that she was actually working in the hospital, she found that time after time, when she was dealing with a patient, she would find herself remembering a point Rob Martin had made in a lecture, something he had discussed that she now found had immediate and practical application.

As a very new student midwife, she didn't yet carry complete responsibility for patients, but she was expected more and more to put her theory into practice.

Checking the foetal heartbeats one morning, under Sister Gray's supervision, Joanna reached her third 'lady in waiting', and found that this baby's heartbeat had become slower. For a moment, her eyes met Sister Gray's and she had to stop herself from saying aloud the words—foetal distress—and from showing her alarm.

'I know you're going to be told this by every one of us,' Rob Martin had said in one lecture, sitting on the edge of the desk and looking at the class of student midwives, his blue eyes for once serious. 'But it's something you can't hear too often. You've got to keep calm in the labour ward in particular. If anything out of the ordinary happens, if you suspect that something might be wrong, don't do or say anything that might panic the patient. Sure, she has to know— but it's important that she's told in a calm and a reassuring manner. So—assess the situation, remember your training, and act accordingly. Foetal distress, now—maybe you've made a mistake, so re-check that heartbeat. If your second reading confirms it, you know what to do.'

Hoping she was giving an impression of calmness and competence and lack of flap, Joanna checked the heartbeat again. She had been right, it had slowed down. It was below a hundred and twenty beats a minute. You know what to do, Rob had said.

And I do, Joanna realised with an upsurge of confidence.

She smiled reassuringly at the patient, then she looked at Sister Gray.

'Yes, Nurse?' the older woman asked, and Joanna saw that she had understood. 'What would you suggest?'

'I think we should stop the oxytocin drip, but leave the I.V. fluid,' said Joanna, and saw the approval in Sister Gray's eyes. 'Mrs Harris, I'd like to help you to lie on your side—that's better. Are you comfortable like that?'

'Yes, thank you, Nurse.'

There was no anxiety in the grey eyes looking up at her, and Joanna knew that thanks to remembering what Rob had said, she had behaved as a good midwife should. But now, with Sister's help, she had to follow through, and the next stage was not her responsibility.

Sister Gray patted the young patient's shoulder.

'Dr Martin will be on his rounds soon, and he'll be in to have a word with you,' she told her. 'Nurse Winter, I need you in the Duty Room.'

Joanna tidied the bedcovers for young Mrs Harris, and followed Sister out of the ward. By the time she reached the Duty Room, Sister was already speaking on the phone.

'Immediately, if you can, Dr Martin,' she was saying. 'Foetal heartbeat is now—what was your finding, Nurse? Below one-twenty. Yes, that has been done. Thank you, Doctor.'

She put the telephone down and looked at Joanna.

'Good, Nurse Winter,' she said briskly. 'You succeeded in keeping your patient as calm as possible. Reason for turning her on her side?'

'To rectify any vena caval occlusion,' Joanna replied, just as briskly. 'Sister, will she need a Caesarian?'

'Almost certainly,' said Sister Gray. 'Dr Martin will decide, and as soon as he does you can prepare her for theatre. This could be a good chance for you to see your first Caesar, since we're not too busy otherwise. I like my nurses to go in as observers for the first time.'

Five minutes later Rob Martin strode into the ward, his white coat flying. Sister Gray met him and took him to the young mother-to-be, and Joanna, accompanying them at Sister Gray's nod, saw that by the time he reached the bed he had somehow managed to change his stride to a saunter.

'How're you doing, Mrs Harris?' he asked, bending over to examine her swiftly, professionally. And thoroughly, Joanna thought with somewhat unwilling admiration, as he straightened up.

'I think this has been going on long enough, Mrs Harris,' he said, his voice quiet and warm. 'This is your first baby, and we do expect a longer labour for a first baby, but we don't let it go on too long. I'm sorry, because I know you were looking forward to a normal birth, but I want to take you into theatre and deliver your baby by Caesarean section right away.'

The young woman's eyes filled with tears.

'Oh, Doctor,' she said shakily, 'I did so want to have my baby naturally. I've been going to classes, and I know all about the breathing and everything. I don't mind—I can take it for longer.'

The tall doctor patted her hand.

'I know,' he said kindly. 'It is disappointing. But it isn't just a case of you being prepared to take it for longer. Your baby is beginning to get a little tired, and that's why we're going to help him on his way.' He turned to Sister Gray. 'Theatre ready, Sister? Then we'll go ahead.'

Joanna had done two months in theatre as part of her general training, and it was strange, now, to be gowned and in the theatre, to see all the activity and not be a part of it. Not yet, she reminded herself. Next time I'll be taking part.

The green-gowned figures moved swiftly around her, and she thought, as she had so often done in general theatre work, that this was real teamwork.

Each and every person seemed to know precisely what to do. The trolley was wheeled in, and Joanna, from her tucked-away corner, could see that Mrs Harris was already drowsy. The anaesthetist moved towards her, and five minutes later the theatre doors swung open and Rob Martin came in, backwards, his gloved hands held high, his mask already in place.

'Everything ready?' he asked, brisk and professional even muffled by the mask. 'Right—scalpel, Nurse.'

He had a quick word with the anaesthetist, nodded his approval, and then, with his scalpel raised, he looked across at Sister Gray.

'Any medical students in today, Sister?' he asked her. 'No? Any of your girls observing? Then let her near enough to see, so she can be useful next time. All right, Nurse, that's near enough—you're not sterile. Can you see?'

Joanna wasn't sure if he recognised her, but she nodded, and he went ahead. From the first incision to the moment when the uterus was exposed and the baby taken out, it was unbelievably quick. She had been told that, and she knew that it had to be done that way, for the sake of the child and the mother, but she found it even more impressive than she had expected. Within five minutes, she was sure, the baby had been handed to the waiting nurse, and the first deep stitches were being done to close the wound. Joanna could see Rob Martin's hands moving swiftly, efficiently, and a few moments later he stood back, and she saw the neat stitching of the final layer.

'Baby all right?' he asked then, turning round.

Everyone in the theatre, Joanna had noticed, had

paused for a relieved fraction of a moment at the baby's first cries, before returning to what had to be done for the young mother. Now the nurse who had taken the baby as soon as he was delivered looked up from the receiving cot.

'He's fine, Dr Martin,' she said. 'Colour good, breathing normal, no further signs of distress.'

'Looks as if we got him out in good time,' Rob Martin remarked to Sister Gray. 'I'd still like to see the paediatrician's report as soon as it comes in. Thanks, girls.'

Joanna, amused, saw Sister Gray, who was certainly old enough to be his mother, blush with pleasure at this, and then, with unconvincing annoyance, frown as Rob strode out, throwing his rubber gloves on the floor.

'He's the most untidy doctor I've ever known, and I've known some,' she commented.

One of the younger Sisters laughed.

'And we all tidy up after him without too many complaints, don't we?' she said, picking up the used rubber gloves and putting them in the rubbish disposal where Rob could just as easily have put them himself.

Not me, Joanna promised herself silently. I'll do what I'm supposed to do for him or for any other doctor, but it's more than time Dr Rob Martin realised that the nursing staff has more to do than tidy up after him! They spoil him, all of them, and for sure he doesn't need any of that, he has a good enough opinion of himself already.

Not, she had to admit, as a doctor. The young nurses had an expression they used of any doctor with an inflated opinion of himself—Big Doctor, they would say disparagingly. Rob Martin, as a doctor, couldn't be accused of that.

No, she couldn't fault him as a doctor—but he certainly does, she told herself from time to time, think he's the answer to a nurse's prayer. And I can't stand men who think girls are just ready to fall at their feet. All right, he's good-looking, but that doesn't make him John Travolta.

'Surely he isn't that bad,' Cathy protested when Joanna said as much to her, as they were making garlic bread for their party. 'I haven't actually spoken to him, but I've seen him around, and he gave us a lecture at college—I thought he was rather nice.'

'That's the whole trouble—that's exactly how he expects every nurse to feel!' Joanna told her, fiercely buttering the loaf she was working on.

Cathy burst out laughing.

'It must be a shock to his system when he meets one like you,' she returned. 'I do look forward to meeting him tonight.'

Joanna shrugged. 'I certainly couldn't care less whether he comes or not,' she said. 'Maybe he'll be on call and some emergency will keep him away.'

The thought of an emergency keeping Rob Martin away came to her mind a little later, as she rushed out of the bathroom, a towel wrapped around her, to finish getting ready.

'Bathroom's free, Lynn,' she called, and Lynn hurried out, also wrapped in a towel.

'About time! I'll never be ready, and Michael is one of these Irishmen who likes parties so much he's sure to be here early.'

Her voice floated through the open bathroom door, accompanied by sounds of vigorous splashing. Joanna, stepping into her dress, thought with gratitude and affection of Cathy, dressed and back in the kitchen doing the finishing touches.

I didn't really need a new dress for tonight, she thought, a little guiltily. She had justified it on the grounds that once Colin got back, there would probably be lots of things going on—not that she could complain of leading a secluded life while he was away, but there would be a few semi-official things connected with the hospital, things that would need a dress like this one.

She zipped it up and stood in front of the mirror to see if she could get away with not wearing a petticoat. Maybe a little see-through, but the lights would be dim, and the soft sea-green material fell so softly, it really would be a pity to spoil the line.

Hair up or down? She pinned it up, and looked critically at herself. She'd worn it up to that other party, when she had sat on a bench with Rob Martin in the garden, and he had kissed her.

Hair down, she decided, telling herself that it must have been the hot bath that had made her cheeks so pink, because she certainly wasn't getting hot and bothered at the memory of a very smooth doctor operating in style!

The doorbell rang, and there was a shriek from Lynn, still obviously in the bath.

'If it's Michael, take him right through, stat!' she called.

Joanna, reaching the door at the same time as Cathy, laughed, because already it was too late; the door had opened and a dark-haired young man had walked in.

'Well now, you must be Joanna, and the little fair one would be Cathy, and of course I'm Michael. The flowers are for the three of you, and I'm sorry I'm early but Lynn said I could be helping with the drinks.'

Oozing Irish charm, Lynn had said, and she was right, Joanna thought, as she and Cathy looked at each other over the huge bunch of flowers.

'How lovely,' she smiled, 'and none of us had time to get flowers. Lynn won't be long—'

She stopped, and followed Michael's astonished gaze to the short distance between the bathroom and Lynn's bedroom door, and a fleeting vision of long brown legs, suntanned arms, and a strategically-placed bath towel.

'Won't be long dressing,' she finished quickly.

'Sure and she looks just fine the way she is right now,' Michael murmured appreciatively. 'What I could be seeing of her, I mean.'

Joanna led him through to the lounge.

'There wasn't too much of her you couldn't see,' she observed, liking this young man of Lynn's instantly. And wondering, for a fleeting moment, why she should immediately like one charming young man, and just as immediately dislike and distrust another.

'Looks as if your friend Rob isn't going to make it,' murmured Lynn, an hour later, as they met in the kitchen. 'He did say he was on call. Pity, though—he's a lot of fun.'

'He's your friend, not mine,' Joanna returned.

'You're the one who wanted him invited, remember.'

'Just as well I have some friends around,' Rob Martin said from the open kitchen window. 'Hi, Lynn, sorry I'm late, I've just had twins—my first twins, so I'm in the mood for celebrating.'

By the time Lynn had opened the door, Joanna was able to regain control of herself, and greet him with a casual lift of the hand as Lynn led him through. Joanna would like to have heard about the newly-delivered twins but a streak of perversity made her stay in the kitchen, spreading extra savouries.

Her re-filled tray was ready to take through, but as she turned round, Rob Martin came into the kitchen.

'I'll carry it for you,' he said, taking the tray from her.

'Thanks, but I can manage,' Joanna replied.

There was laughter in his blue eyes. 'You'd better let me take it,' he suggested. 'There's going to be a rush on that tray when you stand there like that in the doorway with the light behind you!'

Colour flooded Joanna's cheeks. The slip she had decided she could do without—here, in the brightly-lit kitchen, it must be all too obvious.

Rob took the tray from her unresisting hands, and set it down.

'It looks very nice,' he told her. 'But I just thought I'd better warn you. I like you in that soft green—you know, of course, that your eyes are exactly the same colour? Yes, I'm sure you do. Funny, though—you have this terrific copper hair, but your skin is much warmer, it isn't the usual pale redhead's skin.'

His hand touched her cheek for a moment, lingering there, and Joanna stepped back hastily.

'That's because I'm not really a redhead,' she told him. 'Most of it's a rinse.'

He threw his head back with a shout of laughter.

'And honest, too,' he managed to say, at last. 'I like you, Joanna Winter, I really do.'

Her cheek still felt warm where he had touched it, and her heart was thudding unevenly. Chemistry, she reminded herself, nothing more.

'I can't say the same,' she replied, her voice clear and cool. 'I really don't have time to waste like this. Why don't you go and find some girl who might be more grateful for your attentions than I am?'

Slowly the laughter left his eyes. He looked down at her for a long time, unsmiling. She hadn't noticed before how hard the line of his jaw could be, she thought, a little dismayed now.

'I'll do just that,' he said, very quietly. 'I certainly have no intention of hanging around when I'm not wanted.'

And he turned on his heel and walked away from her.

CHAPTER FIVE

It would have been just fine, Joanna thought later, if only he had chosen someone other than Cathy.

She saw him with the younger girl as soon as she took the tray of snacks through. And that wasn't immediately, because she had to stand in the kitchen and take a few deep, calming breaths. Ridiculous, she told herself, the effect that man had on her. Ridiculous, too, to let herself become as infuriated, she knew that.

He was sitting on the couch beside the window with Cathy. They were talking. Or rather, Joanna told herself, Rob was talking, and Cathy was listening, her face upturned to his. Just the sort of audience he likes, Joanna told herself, captive and rapt. She was determined to take no notice.

But as the evening wore on, and he and Cathy stayed together, she found that she couldn't ignore the uneasiness she felt. Cathy, young and gentle and impressionable, was no match for a man like Rob Martin. He would make mincemeat of her in no time at all.

She looked for Lynn, for help, but Lynn and Michael were sitting on cushions in the far corner of the room, and it would have taken an earthquake, Joanna thought, to have disturbed them.

She took a deep breath and walked across the room.

'Cathy,' she said brightly, 'you must come and talk to Donald and Tracy, they're going to have a week's holiday in the Eastern Transvaal, and you can tell them about all these super nature trails you did from that camp—what was it called? Blydepoort?' She took Cathy's hands and drew her to her feet. 'And tell them all you did at Pilgrim's Rest, they'll be near enough to go there too.'

And talking all the time, she led the bewildered Cathy across to one of the groups of people. Only when she had seen Cathy sit down and begin replying to the questions did she feel she could relax, and slip quietly out of the open door to the big airy stoep.

From inside the room she could hear the rise and fall of voices, and once Cathy's laughter, a little shy, but definitely laughter. After all, she reminded herself reasonably, we did have this party so that Cathy could get to know a few other people—not sit in a corner all night with someone like Rob Martin.

The night air was pleasantly cool, and she closed her eyes, realising suddenly, and somewhat to her surprise, just how tense she had been feeling.

'And now,' said Rob Martin, so close to her that she jumped, and her eyes flew open, 'I want a word with you.'

His blue eyes were very dark, and the line of his jaw was very hard. He was extremely angry, Joanna realised, with dismay.

'I don't know what you're talking about,' she said quickly. 'I just—'

His hand closed around her wrist, hard, keeping her from moving away from him.

'You know,' he told her brusquely. 'You know very

well. But let me spell it out for you. You were rescuing Cathy from me. I don't know what you thought I planned on doing to her, right there with all these people there, but maybe you can clear that up for me?'

The cool hostility in his voice was more alarming than open anger would have been.

'Well?' he asked, looking down at her.

Joanna jerked her wrist, but his grip was too firm, and she was forced to remain there.

'Cathy is young and impressionable, and—and gentle,' she said to him, furious to find her voice was less than steady. 'She already thinks you're pretty marvellous as a doctor and as a lecturer, and given half a chance she's likely to fall for you in a big way. And—and—'

'And you were saving her from that?' he asked her.

Anger flooded her.

'Yes, I was,' she told him clearly, lifting her chin. 'I'm too fond of Cathy to stand by and see that happening.'

Very deliberately, he released her wrist.

'I could tell you,' he said, his voice remote, 'that Cathy reminds me of my sister. But I don't expect you to believe that, Joanna, because you have for some reason made up your mind about the kind of man I am, and nothing is going to make you change your opinion. You reckon I'm some sort of second-rate Casanova who preys on young nurses and then casts them aside. I'm not about to justify myself to you, but I'm no heartbreaker. Sure, I've had fun, but so have the girls I've gone around with. I haven't broken any hearts.'

In the darkness of the stoep he was very close to her. Close, and yet a thousand miles away.

'I thought you and I could have had fun,' he said evenly. 'That was all. Sure, you told me you're engaged, but you don't wear a ring, and I didn't get any impression of a girl with eyes and heart for only one man. If I had, I would have left you alone. As I certainly will from now on.' At the open door, he turned. 'Thanks for the party,' he said, impersonally, coolly.

Joanna stayed outside in the cool darkness until she felt the colour in her cheeks subside. Detestable man! she told herself angrily. I certainly don't need a man like that in my life!

And of course, she reminded herself hastily, I certainly won't have one, because Rob Martin will be as good as his word.

She was right about that. Any time they met in the hospital, he was scrupulously polite and correctly professional, treating her exactly as her lowly position as a student midwife demanded.

At the same time, she had to admit, with reluctance, that he didn't go out of his way to be unpleasant to her. Once, when she was assisting when he examined a patient, she dropped a dressing from the sterile tray. Scarlet with embarrassment, she mumbled an apology, expecting him to wither her with a sarcastic remark.

'It's all right, Nurse—just give me another dressing,' he replied, and she saw that in fact all his concern was for the patient he was examining, he had no intention of wasting time or energy on making her feel any smaller than she already did.

They were exceptionally busy in Labour Ward, and she was glad of that, for she found the work here in the maternity hospital fulfilling and absorbing, and she was determined to do well with her training and in her exams.

'It isn't really long enough, this six months' integrated midder, is it?' she said to Lynn one evening as she sat studying her copy of Maggie Myles. 'There's so much to learn—and so much that could go wrong! And I haven't even delivered my first baby yet!'

Lynn, already qualified in midwifery, looked up from the letter she was writing.

'You should stay on for at least another six months after the exam,' she suggested. 'I found that was when everything really came together—especially getting experience out on District. How much longer do you have in Labour?'

'Only a week,' Joanna told her. 'Then I'm in ICU— I'm dreading looking after these tiny babies in Intensive Care, I'm sure I'll feel so helpless.'

'You'll be all right,' Lynn said reassuringly. 'But I hope you get your first delivery before then—it's quite something.'

Joanna knew in theory what she had to do, and she just hoped that when the time arrived she would be able to cope. Two days later it looked as if her big moment had arrived, when Sister Gray asked her to special a patient who had come in during the night.

'Waters broken, fairly strong contractions when she came in, but then everything stopped,' Sister Gray told her, as she and Joanna stood in the Duty Room. 'Naturally, Mrs Turner is a little discouraged now—says she wants to go home, but this is her third baby, and when it comes, it won't waste much time. Dr Walters doesn't want to set up a drip yet—if nothing has happened by four, he'll set one up then. He wants her specialled because the baby is breech— he's already turned it, but back it went, so he's going to turn it again this morning. He's remarkably successful with turning breech babies, Nurse.'

Joanna coloured; she hadn't intended her doubts to show so clearly.

'I know,' Sister Gray went on equably, 'we don't usually turn this late. But this should be successful, although I say the waters are broken, there's still plenty of fluid.' She smiled. 'I hope it's successful, Nurse, for your sake too.'

Joanna knew very well that if the baby remained breech, there would be no question of her doing the delivery, for there could be considerable risk to the unborn baby in a breech presentation. As she hurried along the corridor to her patient, she mentally ticked off the possibilities. Intra-cranial damage, hypoxia, venous congestion, cord compression.

But slowly, as the morning progressed, and she remained with her patient, the textbook words, the carefully-learned medical terms, became real and close. Mrs Turner was a young woman in her mid-twenties—not so much older than I am, Joanna found herself thinking as she rubbed the woman's back to ease the pain after the contractions had started again. She had two little girls, and she and her husband very much wanted a son.

'I do hope nothing goes wrong, Nurse,' she said, her eyes shadowed. 'We've pretty well decided I'll have my tubes tied now, but we never thought of anything going wrong, it wasn't like this with the girls, they were quick, both of them.'

'Nothing is going to go wrong, Mrs Turner,' Joanna reassured her. 'Your baby's heartbeat is good and strong—boy or girl.' She looked at her watch. 'I expect Dr Walters will be in pretty soon to have a look at you, Sister has let him know that your contractions have started again.'

Dr Walters, who was Rob's Martin's chief, came in half an hour later, and although Joanna knew she might have expected it, she was still a little taken aback to find Rob with him.

'Hello, Mrs Turner—Nurse. I brought Dr Martin along with me in case he steps in at the last minute,' the elderly doctor told her, and Joanna saw that even as he was speaking, his voice easy and friendly, his keen grey eyes were assessing the young woman's condition. 'Baby all right, Nurse?'

'Yes, Dr Walters, a good strong heartbeat.' She hesitated, but only for a moment. Maybe she was sticking her neck out, and of course he would find out for himself, but, 'Just before you came in, the baby was very active. I was about to examine Mrs Turner again, because I think it's no longer a breech presentation.'

Dr Walters shot her a keen glance, then bent to examine his patient, gently, expertly, and she knew that she had been right, even before he said anything, as he gave Rob a swift, almost imperceptible nod.

'See that, Rob?' he said. 'The little blighter has done it, just at the last minute—after giving us all a bit of concern. Mrs Turner, your baby is now head down, and it isn't going to be too long.'

'Oh, Nurse, then you will be able to deliver it,' the young woman in the bed smiled, turning to Joanna. 'It will be Nurse Winter's first delivery, Dr Walters, and she couldn't do it if it was breech. Oh, I am glad, Nurse!'

There was another contraction then, a good strong one, and Joanna rubbed the patient's back as she timed it.

'I'll see you in the delivery room before too long, my dear,' the grey-haired doctor said, patting the young woman's shoulder. 'And you too, Nurse.'

'Thank you, Dr Walters,' Joanna murmured, and then, because after all she was a nurse, and he was one of the attending doctors, 'Thank you, Dr Martin.'

An hour later, when it was time for Joanna to go off for lunch, Ellen Turner's contractions were still strong, but no closer together.

'I really don't mind missing lunch, Sister,' Joanna protested.

Sister Gray shook her head.

'You know my rules, Nurse Winter,' she said firmly. 'None of my nurses miss meals. You need the break, and you need to stock up on energy again.' She patted the patient's hand. 'It looks as if Mrs Turner isn't in too much of a hurry, I'm sure she'll be waiting for you when you come back on duty in an hour. Nurse Graham will take over from you, Nurse Winter.'

With more than a little reluctance, Joanna left her patient and went off to lunch. She was always surprised at how hungry she was in the middle of a working day, and she had to admit, as she finished her coffee, that Sister was right, she did feel the better for the lunch break. She looked at her watch, and although she was early, decided to go back to the ward. The nurse who had taken over from her was her friend Tracey, and she would hand over again, knowing that this was to be Joanna's first delivery.

But Mrs Turner's bed was empty, and the patient in the next bed said cheerfully that she had gone to the Delivery Room.

'Must be half an hour ago, Nurse—she's probably had the baby by now.'

She probably has, Joanna thought, as she hurried along the polished corridor to the Delivery Room. All this time, and I've missed delivering the baby.

At the door, she bumped into a tall figure coming out.

'Careful, Nurse,' said Rob Martin, his hand on her arm as she almost lost her balance. And then, the warmth of his voice cooling as he recognised her, 'Oh—Nurse Winter.'

But Joanna had other things on her mind, and she wasn't to be sidetracked.

'Mrs Turner,' she said breathlessly. 'Has she had her baby? Am I in time?'

She thought, afterwards, that a momentary sympathy replaced the coolness in his eyes.

'I've just delivered the baby,' he told her. 'Well, ten minutes ago. Everything happened very quickly at the end.'

With an effort, Joanna put her own disappointment out of her mind. 'Is everything all right?' she asked him. 'Has she got her son?'

He nodded. 'Everything is fine—an easy delivery, and a boy.'

For a moment she thought he was going to say something else, but he only nodded again, briefly, dismissively, and walked on. Joanna turned and went slowly back to the ward, her cheeks scarlet now at the realisation that there she had been cross-examining a registrar as if he was a medical student. And not just any registrar, but Rob Martin.

But I did want to know how things had gone, and if the baby was all right, she told herself, with as much conviction as she could.

'I'm sorry you weren't there to deliver my Peter,' Ellen Turner said later, when Joanna went to see her. 'But it was all so quick—they only just got that nice young doctor in time.' She looked proudly at the baby in his cot beside her bed. 'I'm so glad I've got my boy, Nurse—you'll see, he's just like his daddy!'

'I'm pleased too, Mrs Turner,' Joanna said, but the thought was still there—But I wish you could have waited just a little longer, to let me get my first delivery, because I've only got two more days on Labour Ward! And of course, as she knew all too well, she wasn't the only one waiting anxiously for deliveries—the medical students, as well as the young nurses, had their quota of deliveries, and there was a good deal of fairly friendly rivalry.

'You'll have plenty of deliveries when you're on district,' Lynn comforted her, and Joanna knew that was true, but somehow she wanted to get this first delivery done, so that she could really regard herself as a student midwife.

Her last day on Labour Ward was extremely busy, but it didn't look as if she was to have the chance of that delivery, she found herself thinking as the morning wore on. There were three elective Caesars, and of the normal births, at least three medical students waiting hopefully.

She had just finished preparing one of the Caesarian patients, when there was a message for her to report to Sister Gray. Joanna finished what she was doing, then went to the Duty Room.

'Ah, Nurse Winter,' said Sister Gray, looking up. 'If you go to the Delivery Room right away, you might get your delivery.'

Joanna, unable to believe her good fortune, hurried along the corridor. The doctor standing beside the patient looked up as she went in.

'Ah, Nurse Winter,' said Rob Martin, and came over to her, lowering his voice as he reached her. 'Scrub up, and get your gloves on. This is a normal delivery, but it's going to be quick.'

There was no time to think, no time even to wonder at him thinking of her disappointment the other day and giving her this chance. She eased her fingers into the tight rubber of the gloves and hurried over to the bed. Already the baby's head was showing, and there was no time for panic, no time to wonder if she would remember what she had to do. Gently, she held the baby's head and eased it out, and then, with a sudden slippery movement, the shoulders followed and the baby was born. Triumphant, Joanna held up the baby girl, and just for a moment, Rob Martin's eyes met hers, above their masks. Then the staff midwife took the baby from her, and Joanna had to return her attention to the mother, waiting for the contraction that would deliver the placenta. Only when she had cleaned her patient up could she turn again to have a

look at 'her' baby. There had been one or two surprisingly loud cries, showing the strength of the baby's
lungs, but now she lay peaceful, and although Joanna
knew perfectly well that a newly-born baby couldn't
see, it did seem to her that the tiny baby looked at her,
as she lifted her to take her over to her mother.

'She's a lovely baby,' Joanna said, meaning it, for
now that the initial angry redness had left the baby
girl's face, she could see the perfect tiny features, and
already the soft hair was drying, and showing itself to
be fair, like the mother's. 'What are you going to call
her?'

'Katherine,' the young mother told her, looking
down at her baby. 'But we haven't got a middle name
for her. What's your name, Nurse?'

'Joanna,' said Rob Martin, unexpectedly. 'Katherine
Joanna—that sounds nice, doesn't it?'

Startled, Joanna looked at him, but his attention
was only for his patient, and when, a moment or two
later, his eyes met hers, they held nothing but the cool
distance that had now replaced the laughing warmth
she suddenly, and stabbingly, remembered.

Not that she had any regrets, she told herself
hastily. Really, it was just as well to get things
straight. All right, perhaps she had judged him a little
harshly—I haven't broken any hearts, he had said.
And I thought you and I could have had fun. He
had sounded as if he meant that, she found herself
thinking. But of course, his sort always did sound
convincing.

And certainly, she told herself firmly, she wasn't
going to waste any time thinking of Rob Martin, with
Colin's arrival so close. Fortunately she had managed

to change her day off so that she could be at the airport to meet him.

In the first weeks after he left she had often thought of how it would be, meeting him again, welcoming him back. Now, suddenly, the weeks and the months had gone, and here she was dressing to drive out to meet him—and wondering, as she looked at herself in the mirror, if she had changed, in this year they had been apart. And if he had.

She stood in her bra and briefs, wondering what to wear, realising that she really did look quite different now that she had grown her hair. It had been short and curly all the time Colin had known her. Now it was longer, and with only a soft curl. And copper-coloured, of course—and there was a moment's swiftly-suppressed memory of Rob Martin's touch on her cheek, and his comment on her warm brown skin. Unusual for a redhead, he had said.

Get out of my mind, she told him silently, and she reached into her wardrobe and took out a blue cotton dress that had been a favourite of Colin's.

'Better hurry, Joanna, you don't want to be late,' said Cathy, from the door. 'I phoned the airport for you, and the Jo'burg plane is on time. Nice dress—I don't think I've seen it,' she added.

'Zip me up, please,' Joanna said breathlessly, turning her back to her friend. 'No, it's one I wore a lot before—Colin always liked it.'

'So you're putting the clock back for him, are you?' asked Cathy.

Am I? Joanna wondered as she drove out the airport road. Am I trying to pretend this year hasn't happened? Is that why I chose this dress to wear?

Nonsense, she told herself firmly, parking outside the Domestic Arrivals and half running across to the entrance, as she could see that the jumbo jet had landed. It's much simpler than that—Colin liked to see me in this dress, and I want him to like seeing me again.

The passengers were already filing through, and she looked around, hoping she hadn't missed him. No, there he was, just coming through now. And a wave of relief flooded her whole body. He hadn't changed, not at all. The same Colin—dark hair, a little untidy, and dark eyes, smiling at her now across the crowded airport lounge.

He put down his briefcase and stood waiting for her, his arms held out. And Joanna, after only a moment's hesitation, went right into his waiting arms.

CHAPTER SIX

AFTERWARDS Joanna was to remember, and to hold on to, the overwhelming feeling of familiarity about Colin's arms around her.

There was nothing strange about this man, this was Colin, and the warmth of her own complete recognition of him, the relief of finding it was no difficult and strange thing to be in his arms, made her think how foolish she had been to have had these moments of doubt.

He held her back and studied her.

'It's so good to be back with you, Joanna, you don't know just how good,' he smiled, and kissed her—a warm and affectionate kiss, but brief and un-demanding. 'Missed me?'

'Of course I have,' she said, and it was true. Often, especially in the first months, she had wanted to tell him something, to share something with him, something that just wouldn't have the same impact by letter.

She linked her arm through his and they went to collect his suitcase.

'Just one?' she teased him. 'After all this time? I bet you've come back with exactly the same clothes you took away!'

'I probably have,' Colin agreed, smiling, as he loaded his suitcase on to a trolley.

Outside the big doors he stopped and looked at the mountain.

'You should have seen all the returning South Africans falling over each other to get the first glimpse of Table Mountain,' he told her. 'You know, Joanna, I believe I missed that chunk of mountain as much as I missed anything.'

'Even me?' asked Joanna, safe and secure in the relief of finding that Colin was no stranger, but just—Colin.

'Maybe even you,' he agreed. 'Heavens, is this car of yours still on the road? I thought it would have fallen apart! Is it going to get us back in to Cape Town?'

'Just for that,' she said, getting in behind the wheel, 'you're going to have to put up with my driving. Where to? Right to the hospital? You did say your folks aren't expecting you until tomorrow.'

During the time Colin had been away, his parents had retired from Durban to Hermanus, a small seaside town about two hours' drive from Cape Town.

'I'll take my stuff to the doctor's bungalow tonight,' he said, getting in beside her. 'But I wondered—Joanna, how about going up to Rhodes Mem. to have tea and scones? It's one of the things I've so often thought about doing.'

The small tea-room at the memorial to Cecil John Rhodes, high on the slopes of the mountain, above the hospital, had been a favourite place of theirs in the time they had known each other. It was there, Joanna remembered, that Colin had first told her of his opportunity to go to America.

'Yes, let's do that,' she agreed. 'And if we're really

generous, we can save a few crumbs from our scones for the buck—they're as tame as ever.'

It was March, and there was just a hint of the coming autumn in the air, as they left the car and climbed the stone steps to the almost deserted little tea-room.

'I like this place in the middle of the week,' Colin remarked. 'No students, either medical or university.'

'I'm a student again,' Joanna reminded him, as they sat down.

'Tell me how it's going,' he asked her, when they had ordered tea and scones. 'Had your first baby yet?'

For one swift, disconcerting moment, there was the memory of Rob Martin's eyes meeting hers above his mask, as she held the newly-delivered baby girl in her arms.

'Yes, I have,' she said quickly, pushing the memory away, and she began to tell him about her training, about the things she had already learned and done. He told her about the research he had been working on, in more detail than he had done in letters, and they talked about how lucky he was to get the chance to come back now to do further research in the huge hospital spread out below them.

'How are you going to get to Hermanus tomorrow?' Joanna asked then. 'Is your father driving through for you?'

Colin shook his head.

'I'll hire a car—I must see about buying one pretty quickly, but I'll do that after I get back.' He put his hand over hers. 'You haven't been able to swing it for the weekend? To come with me to Hermanus, I mean—my parents are longing to meet you.'

Joanna shook her head.

'No, I had last weekend off, I couldn't switch,' she said, knowing she wasn't being entirely truthful, knowing she hadn't done more than make a token attempt to change. 'Besides, I do think you should have this time alone with your people, after all this time,' she went on, meaning it—but knowing, as she said it, that she had felt a certain reluctance to be taken to Colin's parents right away, as soon as he arrived, as if—as if she had a right to be there.

They left the tea-room and wandered back down to the car park, then on to the slopes where the buck wandered, free and tame.

'Do you remember that picture I took of you, feeding two of them at once?' asked Colin, and there was something in his dark eyes that made Joanna all at once uncomfortable. 'That was our last visit up here— did I tell you I'd had that picture enlarged and framed? It's been sitting on my desk all the time, and when I've been lonely I've looked at you, smiling at me, and I've thought of you here in Cape Town, waiting for me.'

Waiting for me. They had spoken of that sort of thing before he left, so there was no reason why she should feel a sudden panic, no reason at all, Joanna told herself.

He took her hand in his.

'Small brown hand,' he said softly. 'Small, to belong to such a good and capable nurse. Joanna—'

He put both hands on her shoulders and turned her towards him. Gently at first, and then not so gently, he kissed her. It was a warm and a loving kiss, and Joanna knew that she kissed him back just as warmly, just as lovingly. And then, as his lips became more demanding, she found that she was instinctively drawing back—and remembering, with a pang of disloyalty, that there had been no thought of drawing back from Rob Martin's kiss, no thought of anything but the singing response of her body to his.

Colin's lips left hers, slowly, and he looked down at her, an unasked question in his eyes.

'It—it's quite a time, a year,' Joanna said quickly. 'We need time to get used to each other again.' Her voice was deliberately light.

'Yes, of course you're right. I suppose we do,' agreed Colin, after a moment, and she knew he was hiding his disappointment. He smiled down at her. 'Well, am I taking you out to our old favourite pizza place tonight, or do you want something more special?'

He took her hand in his as they walked back down to the car, but lightly, easily, and soon the slight awkwardness was gone and they were talking in the old way.

They drove to the bungalow at the hospital first, to leave Colin's suitcase, and then to Joanna's flat.

'Nice that you're sharing with Lynn, I've forgotten who the other one is,' Colin said, as Joanna brought coffee through for them.

'Cathy—she's a couple of years younger than Lynn and me, just coming up to her finals. You'll like her,' Joanna told him.

A little while later, listening to Colin and Cathy talking, seeing Cathy's rare and very sweet smile as she replied to Colin's questions, Joanna told herself, not for the first time, what a really dear man Colin was. Kind and thoughtful and friendly—I'm very lucky, she told herself, to be his girl.

In her usual hurricane fashion, Lynn came home then, talking as she opened the door, beginning to throw her bag and her uniform anywhere she could.

'Hi, Colin,' she called, not at all embarrassed to see him there as she hurried into her room, unbuttoning her uniform as she went. 'Sorry, but I'm in a tearing hurry.' A moment later her head appeared round the door. 'Cathy, do you feel like being an angel and running a bath for me? Just a very quick one, Michael will be here soon.'

'Michael'? asked Colin, as Cathy went off to run Lynn's bath.

'The new man in Lynn's life,' Joanna explained. 'He's nice—and he isn't a doctor, he teaches art.'

Colin smiled. 'In all the time I've known Lynn—and come to think of it, I've known her longer than I've known you—there's always been a new man in her life. I think she thrives on change.'

Joanna had been thinking about Lynn and Michael, on and off, in the past few days.

'I have a feeling this might be it,' she said, as much to herself as to Colin. 'There's something—different—about Lynn, this time.'

Colin covered her hand with his own.

'Something different?' he queried. 'You mean—something like we have, you and I?'

This was dangerous ground, although Joanna wasn't prepared to go too deeply into her realisation that it was.

'I'm talking through my hat,' she said quickly. 'This

will probably run its course too, and Lynn will have another new man in her life.'

Cathy came back then, with the coffee pot refilled.

'Are you and Colin having supper here?' she asked Joanna.

Joanna shook her head.

'We're going for a pizza,' she explained. And then, on an impulse that she was to ask herself about, later, 'Want to come with us?'

For a moment Colin's dark eyes met hers, surprised, and—yes, hurt. But Cathy shook her head.

'I have studying to do,' she said. 'And I was counting on a nice quiet evening, with both you and Lynn out.' She stood up and put the mugs on the tray. 'I'm glad to meet you, Colin,' she said, a little shyly. 'All the time I've known Joanna, you've been just a photograph in her room, and now you're real.'

'Nice kid,' Colin observed, when she had gone out. 'Quiet, but nice.'

'She's usually pretty shy,' Joanna told him. 'In fact, I've seldom seen her as relaxed with anyone as she was with you.'

Except, the sudden thought came, with Rob, the other night.

She stood up. 'Let's go,' she said brightly, and held her hand out to Colin.

At the door, they met Michael. Joanna introduced the two men, and told Michael that Lynn was almost ready.

'That means I'll be having time to read the evening paper while I'm waiting,' the Irishman commented, but he was smiling. 'Colin—Joanna, I would say let's make a foursome of it tonight, but you'll be wanting the time just for yourselves, so—some other time, we could be doing that.'

Often, in the first weeks, and even months, that Colin was away, Joanna had thought of how it would be, having him back again. There would be so much to talk about, they would both have so much to say, to make up for all the lost time.

And that was true, there was so much news to exchange, so much for her to hear of what Colin had been doing in America. It was, though, she thought later, trying to understand the confusion of her feelings, strange, the two of them sitting there, as they had so often in the past—and as she had so often thought of them doing, while he was away.

Sometimes it seemed to her that they had never been apart, as they talked and laughed together. But at other times she had to make herself remember how she had felt at the airport, and had to make a conscious effort to regain the feeling of recognition and familiarity she had been so conscious of. She almost, she thought in the middle of the night, lying awake, had to remind herself, this is Colin, the man I love, the man I've been waiting for.

And then, a moment later, that strangeness would be gone, and she would wonder why she had been worried. This was Colin, her dear, dear Colin, and the waiting was over at last, and everything was going to be just fine.

When they parted, his goodnight kiss was warm and undemanding, and she was able to return it just as warmly.

'Good night, Joanna,' he said softly, and his arms tightened around her. 'I suppose you're on duty tomorrow at seven—I'll ring you when I get back from Hermanus next week.'

During the few days Colin was with his parents, Joanna started work in the Intensive Care Unit, with the babies who needed special care. She had thought the baby she had delivered was frighteningly tiny, but most of the babies in the ICU were either premature, or had lost birth weight because of various complications after birth and therefore even smaller.

'You'll remember your Maggie Myles, I'm sure, Nurse Winter,' Sister Gray said, when she came in on Joanna's first day in the Unit. 'Tell me about the nursing care in an intensive care unit.'

Joanna had done her revision the night before.

'Skilled, devoted nursing is mandatory,' she answered. 'With intelligent observation and sufficient knowledge to cope with emergencies. Warmth and quietness are essential. Minimal handling with great gentleness is of cardinal importance. Oxygen, which is—'

Sister Gray held up her hand.

'All right, Nurse, I can see that you know it in theory. But this is where you put that theory into practice.' She bent over one of the incubators. 'Baby Ross had asphyxia and a low Agpar score, and he's having assisted ventilation in a Vicker's incubator. This is the neovent, and here are the humidifier and the oxygen analyser. This is the naso-tracheal tube you will learn how to adjust.'

She looked at Joanna.

'That's the medical picture, Nurse. Now, put your hand in and touch him, gently. Don't be afraid, you've got to learn to handle your babies confidently, they're quite incredible at sensing a lack of assurance. Yes, touch his hand.'

The baby was lying in the incubator, and the tube and the catheter, minute as they were, looked so big beside the frail-looking little body. Joanna's heart turned over as she watched the baby's laborious breathing. Gently she put her finger against his hand, and to her surprise, the tiny fingers closed around her own finger with unexpected strength, and she found herself smiling, delighted, willing the tiny baby to go on gaining strength.

'You'll do, Nurse,' Sister Gray said quietly. 'Just feel like that for every one of your babies here.'

That wasn't difficult, Joanna found. Each baby had its own problems, and each baby very quickly became an individual. She hadn't expected this, with such tiny new babies, but the amount of nursing care each one needed meant that the nurses in the ICU spent a great deal of time with each little patient.

She found, too, that Sister Gray was right. The babies did respond to confident handling, and although the handling had to be minimised at first, as each baby improved the nurses were encouraged to hold him or her whenever possible.

Joanna was sitting giving one of the babies his first bottle one day, her head bent in concentration, when the door opened. She knew that someone had come in, but didn't want to take her attention away from the feeding of the baby.

'Is that one of my twins, Nurse?' Rob Martin asked cheerfully. 'How is he doing?' And then, recognising her, 'Oh, Jo—Nurse Winter. I didn't know you were in ICU. Is that one of my twins?'

'Yes, it is, Dr Martin,' Joanna replied, glad that after one glance she could bend over the reluctantly-feeding baby again.

'I'll have a look at his chart,' the doctor said, his voice cool, professional. 'I see his respiration is almost normal now, and I'm happy about the last two temperatures. Little brother has some way to go, though.'

She had seen him with babies before, but never with one as tiny as this, his hand dwarfing the baby in the incubator as he examined him gently.

'Little skinned rabbit,' he said softly, and somehow the warm affection in his voice didn't surprise her. 'You've got to start fighting, like your brother, you hear me?'

He turned away from the incubator and looked at her.

'Ever noticed, Nurse, that some babies are born fighters? This one—' gently, his finger touched the tiny cheek of the baby in her arms—'is one. I'm hoping little brother will decide to be one too. Because you can do as much as medical science knows about for these babies—but you need that fighting spirit, too.'

He had forgotten, she thought, that he was speaking to Joanna Winter, then he suddenly remembered.

'I hear your fiancé has returned,' he said, the warmth gone from his voice.

Deliberately he glanced at her left hand.

'I'm surprise to see no ring yet,' he commented.

And before she could say anything in reply he went out, closing the door behind him.

CHAPTER SEVEN

COLIN's job in the Neurology Department at the huge hospital was even more demanding than he or Joanna had expected. His research was challenging and stimulating, and a logical follow-up on the work he had been doing in America—but it needed, he said ruefully, a great deal of stamina, and a twenty-five-hour day.

'Between my long hours and your off-duty times, we don't seem to get together as much as I thought we would,' he said one night, over Irish coffees at the Pig and Whistle, a favourite student meeting-place near the hospital. 'I'm sorry, love.'

'It's all right, Colin,' said Joanna, meaning it. 'You were very lucky to get the chance to work with Max Johnson, and you must admit you're enjoying it.'

'Oh yes, I'll admit that,' Colin agreed, smiling. 'I've always known that research was my line—my degree was just the way to get there, I never did see myself either in general practice or in hospital work.'

And Rob, Joanna thought involuntarily, would never be right doing anything but working with patients.

'Anyway,' she said quickly, 'it's nice when we can have even a little while like this.'

'It is,' he agreed, but there was a question in his eyes, a question that he hadn't asked, and that she didn't know how she would answer.

I should mind more than I do, she thought later that night, with a disturbing honesty, as she lay in bed unable to sleep. I should want Colin and me to spend much more time together, I shouldn't be—But she turned away from the word that had come into her mind: relieved. No, she told herself quickly, defensively, that wasn't true. She did enjoy being with Colin, as she always had. She liked hearing about his work, and she knew that he was interested in hearing about hers.

We laugh at the same things, we like the same kind of music, we—we get on very well together, she reminded herself.

And that was true.

Just as it was true, she admitted to herself, painfully, that when Colin took her in his arms and kissed her, it was pleasant, and she enjoyed it, but that was all. But perhaps that was the best basis for a good relationship—similar tastes, a warm and steady affection. A pleasant, steady glow, rather than—fireworks.

Fireworks—and a man like Rob Martin.

No, Joanna told herself firmly, that's quite enough.

She got out of bed, went through to the kitchen and made herself a cup of tea, and when she had finished it she managed to put all the disturbing thoughts out of her head and fall asleep. And in the morning, somehow it seemed a little ridiculous that she had allowed herself to think so many strange things. Of course she and Colin were doing just fine, it was only natural that they both needed some time, after this year apart.

I will be positive, she told herself determinedly, as

she put a slice of wholewheat bread into the toaster and switched the kettle on.

'You look bright and cheerful,' commented Cathy, coming into the kitchen, rubbing her eyes.

'I am bright and cheerful,' Joanna replied confidently. 'But why are you up so early—you're off today, aren't you?'

'Oh, things to do,' Cathy said vaguely, and there was something in her voice that made Joanna look at her sharply. With a stab of guilt she realised that she had been somewhat preoccupied with her own affairs recently, and she hadn't been keeping an eye on Cathy, as she had got into the habit of doing.

'Your toast is ready,' said Cathy, handing her the slice of hot toast.

'Thanks,' Joanna replied absently, buttering her toast and making her coffee with one eye, as usual, on the clock, for she was on duty at seven, and that meant being in the Intensive Care Unit a quarter of an hour before that.

'You've been out more than usual, haven't you?' she asked the younger girl.

Cathy's fair hair swung over her face as she cut herself a slice of bread.

'Yes, I suppose I have,' she agreed casually. 'Want any more toast, Joanna?'

'No, thanks,' Joanna replied. 'Cathy, I've been very selfish, too tied up in my own affairs. You've obviously met someone, and neither Lynn nor I has even noticed! Go on, tell me about him. Is he a medical student?'

Cathy turned to face her.

'It isn't like that at all, Joanna,' she said quickly, her

gentle young face flushed. 'This is different—I have
been going out quite a bit, but—but it isn't what you
think. We're just friends.' She smiled shyly. 'He
actually says I'm like a sister to him, and I certainly
look on him as a good friend, just like a brother.'

'He?' Joanna queried tightly, but she knew the
answer even before Cathy replied. 'Who, Cathy?'

'Rob,' Cathy told her. 'Rob Martin. I know he isn't
one of your favourite people, Joanna, but he's so nice,
and so easy to talk to.'

'I can well believe that,' Joanna agreed. She looked
at the clock in despair, knowing that this certainly was
the wrong time to start discussing Rob Martin and his
complete unsuitability even as a friend—a friend!—
for a girl like Cathy.

'Cathy, I'll be late,' she said, rising and carrying her
plate and her mug to the sink. 'But we'll talk about
this again.'

'I'll wash these for you,' the younger girl offered.
'And don't worry about me, Joanna—Rob and I
really are good friends.'

Good friends indeed! Joanna thought sarcastically
as she drove too fast along the almost deserted
Main Road and turned off for the hospital. I just
don't believe Rob Martin could be good friends with
any girl! And especially a defenceless innocent like
Cathy!

But her hostility to Rob Martin the man couldn't be
carried over to Rob Martin the doctor. Working in the
ICU, she saw quite a lot of him, for he was more than
conscientious about the babies in his care. Especially
the twins he had delivered. The bigger one was coming along nicely, but the little one hadn't gained as

much ground as they hoped.

Both babies had been baptised—not, as Rob explained to the young parents kindly, gently, that they thought either baby was in real danger, but often with premature babies in the ICU, parents felt happier to have this done. And so there was a short and moving ceremony one morning, when the young parents' minister baptised the twins, James Kenneth and John Robert.

'Kenneth is after their father,' young Hilary Cooper told Joanna shyly. 'And Robert, of course, is after Dr Martin. He's been so wonderful with the babies—especially with little John.' Her eyes filled with tears. 'It seems so strange, Nurse, for me to be at home, and—and my babies still here. Do you think— are they going to be all right?'

Joanna looked down at tiny John, back in the incubator with the drip in position, and the naso-tracheal tube.

'Everything possible is being done for him, Mrs Cooper,' she said reassuringly. 'He's certainly holding his own.'

But no more than that, she found herself thinking, in the days after her early-morning talk with Cathy. The bigger twin, James, was out of the incubator and would probably be allowed to be taken home very soon. But little John—

'How do you think he's doing, Nurse Winter?' asked Rob Martin, coming in unexpectedly to find her adjusting the humidifier.

Joanna hesitated.

'Everything seems to be fine,' she said, with some reluctance. 'Temperature and respiration are all right, his colour is good, and Dr Ashton came back to check his reflexes.'

'But you're not entirely happy about him,' Rob Martin said, and it wasn't a question.

'No, I'm not,' Joanna admitted, thinking that she must sound very foolish, and yet feeling she had to say this. 'I don't know whether it's just a feeling, or a hunch, or—'

'I prefer to call it intuition,' Rob said quietly. 'And I put a lot of store by it. Most good nurses have it—it goes beyond training and experience, and I trust it. No, I'm not entirely happy about little John, either. Have me called if you feel there's any need to.'

At the door, he turned and smiled.

'And I won't mind if there isn't any real medical justification for your concern,' he told her. 'That feeling is good enough for me.'

That afternoon, just before she was due to go off duty for tea, Joanna, having just checked her babies before handing over to the other student midwife, was actually out in the corridor when she knew she couldn't go off until she had had another look at baby John.

'Forgotten something?' her friend Tracey asked.

Joanna shook her head.

'Not really, I just wanted to check on little John again. I know he was fine, but—'

The baby's skin, pink when she had looked at him, was bluish-grey. He felt cold and limp, and his breath was shallow, with an occasional gasp.

'Call Dr Martin—tell him Baby John has severe asphyxia, ask him to come stat!'

Working swiftly but as gently as possible, she aspirated the pharynx and then the nostrils, using a mucus extractor. Until the doctor came, there was little more she could do other than keep the baby warm.

She heard Rob Martin coming up the stairs, two at a time, then he was in the room, and beside her.

'I'll need a Penlon bag and mask,' he told her. 'Pharynx and nostrils?'

'Aspirated,' she told him, handing him the mask that would deliver pure oxygen to the distressed baby.

'Good girl,' he said, his eyes on the baby as he took the equipment from her. Joanna felt that her own breath almost stopped, as she watched him using the respirator on the tiny baby. It seemed an eternity before he moved the mask from the small face.

'His colour is better already,' murmured Joanna.

'And he's breathing on his own,' Rob agreed, his voice low. 'But it's early to tell. I want him in the incubator, and I want the drip set up, and then I want to sit right here for the next half hour.'

Joanna, her own tea break entirely forgotten, did all that had to be done for the baby, and then, with a quick word of explanation to Sister Gray who was in charge of the nursery, she made coffee and took it in to Rob.

'Thanks, Nurse,' he said, taking the mug of coffee from her, his eyes never leaving the tiny and pathetic form in the incubator. 'I need that.'

But half an hour later he had drunk no more than a mouthful, and the rest was left cold.

'I have to do my rounds,' he said, standing up. 'But I think he'll do. I think he's going to make it.'

He was right—somehow, once the drama was over, the tiny baby began to make real progress, and within a week both he and his brother had left the hospital to be taken home.

Joanna, on reflection, hadn't had the talk with Cathy. Somehow the time had never seemed right, for she had never felt that she could discuss Rob Martin coolly and dispassionately with Cathy. Impressed as she was by his concern and ability as a doctor, she could not accept that away from the hospital he was anything but footloose and fancy-free—and a heartbreaker. But she knew that there was a strong streak of loyalty in Cathy, and if she were to come out too strongly against Rob, the younger girl just might dig in her heels, and Joanna could find that instead of avoiding trouble for Cathy, she had actually precipitated it. So she said nothing.

Off duty at four one day, she came back to the flat, changed into old jeans and a cut-off blue tee-shirt, and washed her hair. She had just finished when the doorbell rang. Cathy or Lynn forgotten the key, Joanna thought, and she tied a towel round her head and padded barefoot through the hall.

Rob Martin stood there, and he was also in old jeans and a tee-shirt. They looked at each other in mutual astonishment.

'I didn't expect to find you here,' said Rob, and she thought, afterwards, that it was probably the first time she had seen him even slightly at a loss.

'I live here,' she pointed out brusquely. 'And I came off duty at four.'

'I have an afternoon off too,' he said, just as brusquely. 'I thought Cathy might be down early from college.'

Joanna took a deep breath. 'Oh yes, I believe you

and Cathy have been seeing each other quite a bit,' she said.

Rob Martin's dark blue eyes narrowed.

'I believe you're right,' he returned, and now his voice was cool and amused. 'What do you plan to do about it, oh guardian of young nurses?'

Joanna wished furiously that she didn't have a large pink towel wound round her head, and that she wasn't barefoot, for the fair-haired man seemed to tower above her.

'I haven't decided,' she said, hoping her voice was as cool as his own. And then, completely untruthfully, 'Actually, I don't think the situation is worth bothering about—sorry you've missed Cathy.'

She turned and went inside, her hand ready to close the door.

Rob Martin's hand over hers stopped her.

'Joanna,' he said, his voice low.

Somehow he was very close to her. Joanna wanted to move away, but she couldn't. Not even when he came closer and looked down at her, unsmiling, while he took her hand from the doorknob and closed it, so that they were in the small entrance hall of the flat.

He kissed her then, as she had known he would from the moment he said her name. His lips were fierce and demanding on hers, and his arms held her captive—if she had wanted to get away. But she didn't. She was to remember, afterwards, how she had clung to him, how everything in her had responded to his body against hers. There was nothing else in the whole world but the two of them.

'Oh, Joanna,' he murmured, his lips still close to her. And slowly, through the singing of her blood and the uneven thudding of her heart, she heard the warm, sleepy amusement in his voice. Amusement— at how easily she had surrendered? And all she knew about this man, all she detested about him, surfaced, and swamped the other, the dangerous feelings.

She drew back from him, and without conscious thought she slapped his face.

He straightened, and in the brown of his face she could see the red imprint of her hand. For a moment she thought he was to turn and walk away without saying anything, but instead, taking her completely by surprise, he kissed her again—a hard, angry kiss that still, to her shame, stirred her, so that in spite of herself she could do nothing but respond.

Then he let her go, so suddenly that she almost fell.

'That proves how right you were, doesn't it?' he said, his voice even and remote. 'No girl should trust me—I'll take advantage of any girl, anywhere, any time. No wonder you feel you should warn all your friends about me!'

CHAPTER EIGHT

THERE was nothing but cool dislike in Rob Martin's blue eyes as he looked down at her.

'You don't believe in giving anyone a chance at all, do you?' he asked. And without giving her any time to reply, even if she had been able to, 'No, when Joanna Winter decides what a person is like, that's it. No second chances—no first chances, come to think of it. Life is going to be tough, Joanna, for someone so sure she's right.'

At the door, he turned and looked back at her.

'Just one thing,' he said evenly. 'I'm not prepared to let you spoil my friendship with Cathy. And I mean friendship, and if you don't believe me—well then, in the immortal words, frankly, my dear, I don't give a damn!'

The door closed behind him and she heard him walk away with long, decided strides.

Joanna had never been a girl who cried easily, but now, to her astonishment, she found there were tears running down her cheeks. Tears of anger, she reminded herself, at the way Rob Martin had spoken to her. Very fitting, really, she told herself as she scrubbed the signs of tears from her face, that he had quoted Rhett Butler, for there was another high-handed, arrogant so-and-so!

She rubbed her hair fiercely until it was almost dry, then combed and pushed it into place, still so angry that she barely glanced in the mirror as she did it.

'Tea,' she said aloud. 'I need a cup of good strong tea!'

She had just made a large pot of tea when Lynn came in.

'I'm dead on my feet,' she announced, sitting down on a kitchen stool. 'Are we fools to stick with this sort of life, Joanna? Do you know, my sister makes twice as much money as I do, she works about half as long, and never nights or weekends, and the biggest occupational risk she has is when she gets up to go to her filing cabinet and her boss pinches her bottom! She just doesn't know she has a back or feet!'

She unlaced her dark blue shoes and eased her feet out of them, wiggling her toes experimentally.

'Still a shade of feeling down there,' she commented. 'Tea—thanks, Joanna, you're an angel.'

It was only when she had taken a few sips of tea that she looked properly at Joanna.

'Something wrong, Jo?' she asked, and the sudden concern in her voice was almost too much for Joanna. 'I don't believe you and Colin have had a row?'

Joanna shook her head. 'It's nothing to do with Colin,' she said, not quite steadily. 'It's—I just had a flaming row with Rob Martin.'

'With Rob Martin?' repeated Lynn, astonished. 'You mean—at the hospital?'

Joanna shook her head. 'No,' she said unhappily. 'I mean right here. He—he came to see Cathy, and I told him—'

She stopped, because in fact she hadn't really told

him anything about how she felt. Not this time, at least.

'I just don't think he's any good for Cathy,' she went on, a little lamely. 'Cathy's young, trusting— innocent, in many ways.'

Lynn put her cup down on the table.

'Joanna, just what do you have against Rob Martin? I've never seen you dislike anyone the way you dislike him.'

Joanna lifted the teapot and refilled both their cups.

'I know he's a buddy of yours,' she said, furious with herself because her voice still wasn't steady. 'But he's just the most arrogant, high-handed man I've ever met. He thinks every nurse should fall at his feet, he thinks a smile or a word from him should guarantee that any girl will just fall into his arms.'

Unbidden, then, there was the searing memory of just how it felt to be in Rob Martin's arms, and she felt her cheeks grow scarlet.

Lynn looked at her, unable to hide her surprise.

'He isn't that bad, Jo,' she said mildly. 'Sure, he has fun, and he does get around, but he's no better and no worse than a lot of men. What about Piet Marais in Radiology? He gets around, and he actually boasts that he's been out with every nurse with a score over seven in Cape Town. I've never heard you go on about him the way you go on about poor old Rob.'

'Poor old Rob,' Joanna told her, 'is more than able to look after himself, I'm sure it doesn't worry him one bit what I think of him!''

And that was true, she told herself defiantly. The only reason he had kissed her, she was certain, was that she represented some sort of challenge to him—

one of the few girls who seemed to be able to resist Dr
Rob Martin's charms. Seemed, she reminded herself
bitterly, because he could have been under no mis-
apprehension about the way she returned his kiss. But
at least she had made it perfectly clear to him that that
was purely a—purely a physical response, and therefore completely meaningless. All right, if you were
going to be completely and clinically honest, he was a
very attractive man, and undoubtedly something a
little peculiar happened when he kissed her, something that could very easily get out of hand. But she
had no intention of letting it get out of hand, no
intention of becoming another scalp for Dr Casanova
Martin. As she had made perfectly clear to him, she
reminded herself, seeing once again the scarlet imprint of her hand on his face. And hearing again the
cool remoteness of his voice, in response to what she
had done.

'Hey, come back, Joanna, you're miles away!'
chided Lynn, concern still in her eyes. 'And you
haven't told me the end of the story—did you persuade our Rob to leave Cathy alone? And if you did,
is Cathy going to thank you for—well, I have to say
it—for interfering?'

Yes, I suppose it is interfering, Joanna thought with
reluctance. But I'm too fond of Cathy just to stand
by—

She said as much to Lynn, and the other girl looked
at her curiously.

'Don't you agree that we have to look after Cathy a
bit?' Joanna asked her.

Lynn shook her head.

'I'm not so sure,' she replied after a moment. 'I

think Cathy is better able to look after herself than we sometimes think. And she says, Joanna, that she and Rob are just friends. That could be true, you know.'

Joanna sniffed.

'You sound just like my Great-aunt Emily,' Lynn told her, diverted. 'I've never heard anyone but her sniff in such a—Victorian way!'

Reluctantly Joanna had to smile.

'Sorry you landed for all this, Lynn,' she said, but the other girl patted her hand.

'That's what friends are for, dear. And you've seen me through many an emotional storm.' Then, suddenly serious, her eyes met Joanna's. 'I'll tell you this, Jo, and then I won't say another word about him. I've never shed any tears over Rob, and I don't know any other girl who has—he's always kept it light, and fun, and we've all known there was nothing serious in it. All right, all right, like I said, no more!' she laughed. 'Tell me what you're wearing to the party on Saturday night. I presume you and Colin are going?'

There was a party arranged to celebrate some of the new hospital appointments, including Colin's.

'Oh yes, we're going,' Joanna replied. 'That's if Colin can tear himself away from his laboratory for the evening! I'm not sure what I'll wear, Lynn—I do have that new greeny dress.'

But even as she said it, she knew all at once that she didn't want to wear the soft sea-green dress she had worn to their own party—the dress Rob had commented on.

'I'll probably wear my pink cotton button-through skirt, it's going to be very casual,' she said quickly.

'Then you can borrow that Greek cotton blouse of

mine, if you like,' offered Lynn. 'And if you're wearing that, could I borrow that brown silky dress of
yours? I couldn't borrow it before, but I have lost a
kilo, and it should look dead right. I think Michael
would you like me in something silky and slinky.'

Joanna stood up. 'Michael would like you in anything, and you know it,' she told her friend affectionately. 'Yes, of course you can borrow it.'

All three of them, it turned out, were going to the
party. Cathy, a little anxiously, told them that she was
going with Rob Martin. Joanna couldn't bring herself
to show any enthusiasm, but she did manage not to
make any adverse comment, and she congratulated
herself on that.

It was Michael's idea that the six of them should go
out for a meal before the party.

'If he'd asked me, I would have put him off,' Lynn
explained the day before the party. 'But he thought it
was a brilliant idea, and he went ahead and rang both
Rob and Colin, and fixed it up. It was—quite enter-
prising of him,' she finished feebly. 'I'm sorry,
Joanna.'

'It's all right,' Joanna said brightly—too brightly,
she knew. 'Good heavens, Lynn, although I can't
stand the man, for the sake of politeness I can put up
with his company for a short time!'

And there was no doubt, she had to admit on
Saturday evening, as the six of them sat having steaks
in the restaurant that overlooked the huge open-air
swimming pool in Seapoint, that Rob Martin could be
entertaining, and good company. Apart from a rather
formal greeting he said nothing to her, and that suited
her very nicely, she told herself more than once.

'The mountain, and the sea, and a good steak,' Colin said contentedly. 'I don't know which I've missed more.'

'What about Joanna?' asked Lynn. 'Or doesn't she come into it?'

Colin put his arm around Joanna's shoulders and drew her close to him for a moment.

'Joanna is in a class by herself,' he said softly. 'You know that, don't you, honey?'

Honey. That was something new, since his year in America. Joanna rather liked it—or she usually did. Tonight, with Rob Martin's dark blue eyes resting thoughtfully on Colin and her, she wasn't so sure.

Rather to her surprise, Colin and Rob got on very well together. There was a great deal Rob wanted to know about hospitals, and the whole system of medical care in America, and although some of his questions were out of Colin's field, he usually had some knowledge.

'I suppose,' Rob said at one point, thoughtfully, 'a doctor is a doctor is a doctor, wherever he is. We tend to hear the bad things about the system, the cases that reach the newspapers, cases of negligence or over-charging, or whatever. But I suppose there are plenty of good and conscientious doctors around, just getting on with their jobs.'

'Nurses, too,' Lynn put in.

'Sure,' Rob agreed, and now he was smiling. 'Ordinary people just getting on with their jobs—and doing them reasonably well, most of the time, like all of us.'

'It's a great place for research, that's for sure,' Colin said then. 'There doesn't seem to be a shortage of funds—usually some company or other will come through with the necessary to let you get on with the job.'

'But you came back,' Michael reminded him, and Colin explained that he had always wanted to work in the Neurology Department, under Max Johnson, and when the chance came up he had to take it. It turned out that Rob knew another of the young doctors working with Colin, and somehow or other, Joanna was never quite sure how it happened, plans were being made for a long walk in the Fernkloof Nature Reserve at Hermanus, where Colin's parents lived.

'Lewis and I have already been talking about doing it,' said Colin enthusiastically. 'We could all go—we just need to coincide the weekend, and you girls could sleep in the house, and there's a loft for us fellows. It will be great fun.'

Just great, thought Joanna, dismayed. She wouldn't be able to refuse to go, because already Colin had been pressing her to come to Hermanus for a weekend. And with Colin and Rob striking up this beautiful friendship, there wouldn't be much chance of avoiding Rob.

'Surely we should be on our way to the party?' she asked. 'It's almost ten—things should be going well now.'

The party was noisy and crowded, and obviously successful. They managed to find a table, and almost immediately Michael and Lynn disappeared. Occasionally Joanna caught a glimpse of her brown silk dress at the far end of the room, but knowing that Michael was as enthusiastic a dancer as Lynn, she thought they'd be lucky to see anything more of the other two.

'Dance, honey?' asked Colin, and she took his hand and joined him in trying to find a few inches of space. A little to her surprise, Rob and Cathy didn't dance, and as Joanna and Colin moved, little by little, around the room, she caught occasional glimpses of them, sitting closer together now, talking mostly, but once she saw Cathy's fair head flung back as she laughed.

'Too crowded for you?' asked Colin as they reached the table again.

'Not really,' Cathy replied. 'But we were talking.'

'Come along, then,' Colin said to her. 'In this noise, dancing is easier on the nerves than talking!'

And they were gone, and Joanna and Rob were left on their own. She looked at him and saw her own wariness mirrored in his eyes, and somehow this made her feel just a little better.

'Good band,' she said loudly, because it seemed foolish to sit there glaring at each other.

'Yes, it is—let's dance,' he replied.

That was the last thing she had intended, but as he was already taking her hands and drawing her to her feet, arguing or refusing would have looked very noticeable. And besides, Joanna told herself, this Beatles revival business was great, *A Hard Day's Night* would keep them well and truly dancing.

But five minutes later the music changed, and Joanna was sure she'd never heard *Yesterday* played quite so slowly. All round them couples were moving closer to each other, dancing slowly and—and smoochily, Joanna thought in dismay.

'Do you want to stop?' Rob Martin asked her, very

politely, and a reviving wave of anger swept through her. Oh no, she thought, I'm not having you think I'm afraid to dance with you, Rob Martin!

'No,' she said clearly. 'Do you?'

Without a word he drew her closer to him. She hadn't danced with him before this, but she had seen him dancing at that first party, and she knew he was a good dancer. What she hadn't realised was that the two of them would dance together as if they had been partnering each other for years.

Once, nervously, she began to say something.

'Don't talk,' he told her brusquely, and she stopped and gave herself up to the pleasure of dancing with a man who really could dance. And that, she told herself, was all there was to it.

Strangely, before the end of *Yesterday*, without a word of explanation, his arms released their hold on her and without a word he led her back to their table.

'Something else to drink?' he asked formally. 'I'll get you some more wine.'

When he returned, Colin and Cathy were with him, Cathy protesting that the music was too good for them to stop.

'Then I'll dance with you, if you've worn Colin out,' said Rob.

When they had moved back into the crowd, Colin turned to Joanna.

'Let's go outside,' he said. 'It's hot and it's noisy.'

Suddenly apprehensive, Joanna replied that it was probably just as noisy outside.

'I want to talk to you,' he said, very firmly.

The music was just a pleasant background when they were outside, and although it was already April, and autumn, the evening was warm. There was a stone wall, and Colin led her to it.

'Sit down, Joanna,' he said, and sat down beside her.

'What a lovely evening,' Joanna said breathlessly. 'Can you think that summer is almost over, it seems—'

Colin took both her hands in his.

'Joanna,' he said quietly, 'stop it. It's time we talked, you and I.'

Joanna looked down at their joined hands. Yes, she thought, I suppose it is.

'Before I went away,' he reminded her, his hands holding hers firmly, 'we talked about getting engaged. We decided, sensibly, that it would be better to wait until I came back. Joanna honey, I've been back for three weeks now. A few times I've tried to raise the question, and you've evaded me. But this time you're not getting away. I'm not going to go down on one knee, but I am going to do the thing properly.'

His hands tightened on hers.

'Will you marry me, Joanna?'

CHAPTER NINE

THE words had been said, and Colin wanted—and deserved—an answer.

'Oh, Colin,' Joanna said, not quite steadily, 'I know this is what we thought before, that we'd get engaged when you came back, but—'

'But?' he repeated, his eyes on her face. He smiled, but she could see that it was an effort. 'I suppose this is where I ask you if there's someone else?'

'No, Colin, there's no one else,' she told him steadily. There isn't anyone in the world, she thought unhappily, I like and admire, and—and get on with more than you, but—She looked at him, and then, with complete honesty, she said, 'I think it's just that I'm not quite ready to get engaged. Couldn't we just wait a bit—go on as we are, and give ourselves time?'

'I don't need time, honey,' he told her. 'But if you do, then yes, we'll go on in the same way, and I'll ask you again before too long.'

Joanna leaned forward and kissed him, over-whelmed with relief at the way he had taken this, and pleased, too, that now they had talked about it and brought it out into the open.

She had meant it to be no more than a light and fleeting kiss, but Colin didn't let her go. His arms closed around her and his lips were warm on hers. It was a pleasant and enjoyable kiss, and Joanna was a little surprised when he let her go, then looked at her, a question in his dark eyes even before he spoke.

'Joanna,' he asked doubtfully. 'Are you—?'

But before he could say any more, she saw a movement in the shadows behind him, and Rob Martin came towards them.

'Sorry to interrupt,' he said, a little brusquely, 'but I was sent to bring you in—Max wants to propose a toast for all the new appointments.'

Colin and Joanna followed him in, and Colin kept her hand in his as they went back into the crowded room. The toasts were proposed, and there were noisy congratulations and a few speeches, then the music began again, and the dancing.

But Joanna couldn't help wondering, then and later, how long Rob Martin had stood there in the shadows when she was in Colin's arms.

With every day that she worked in the Intensive Care Unit, she found that she learned more, and felt more in command of what she was doing. It was satisfying, working in the small unit, with no more than ten babies there, and time for the nurses to give each one the specialised care so necessary. The working day flew by, for every half hour she had to check and record the colour of the babies' lips and tongue, the skin temperature and the incubator temperature, the respiration, and the heart rate. Anything abnormal had to be reported, but at the same time the student midwives had to be able to take immediate action even before a doctor could arrive.

'If the baby develops apnoea,' Sister told Joanna briskly, 'you flick his feet, to stimulate the breathing. If this is ineffective, apply face-mask ventilation until spontaneous breathing recommences, and report the episode.'

It was a word and a condition in the pages of a textbook, until the day Joanna, doing her half-hourly respiration check, saw that one of her babies, a tiny premature girl, lay still and limp, and already a bluish colour. Joanna, standing beside the tiny incubator, thought that her own heart had stopped beating. In that moment, as she stood there in horror, she saw again the young parents, so thrilled to have a little girl after two boys, and so confident that the nurses in the Intensive Care Unit would look after their baby.

Flick her feet, Joanna thought, and if that's ineffective—

Gently but firmly she flicked the tiny feet. For an eternity nothing happened, and then, with a little gasp and a shudder, Baby Robertson began to breathe again. Joanna, weak at the knees, stood beside her, watching, until she was quite certain that the breathing pattern was re-established. Then, her hand still unsteady, she went to write her report.

'She seems to be all right now, anyway,' Rob Martin said later, completing his examination of the baby. 'We've ruled out some of the causes—overheating, infection, hypoglycaemia. Very often, with apnoea, it's almost impossible to detect the cause. I'm hoping, with Baby Robertson, that it won't happen again. If it does, and we're dealing with recurrent apnoea, this is what I want you to watch out for. Check her breathing pattern, and if it becomes progressively more irregular and shallow, she's in trouble. Heart rate—I'm worried if it drops below a hundred per minute. Cyanosis of the mucous membranes. Any or all of these, you send for me immediately.' He turned suddenly from the incubator and looked at her. 'You all right, Nurse?'

The unexpectedness of this took Joanna so much by surprise that she couldn't even attempt to control the rush of warm colour to her face.

'I—yes, thank you, Dr Martin,' she replied. 'It's just that I haven't seen this outside a textbook before, and I thought—'

'You thought she was dead,' Rob said quietly, completely serious. 'I know—I had the same experience when I was an intern. It's terrifying, isn't it?'

'I couldn't believe it, when I flicked her feet and she began to breathe again,' Joanna agreed.

'Doesn't always work, of course,' he commented. 'Then we have to ventilate, suction the airway, and if the attacks persist, we give aminophylline, which stimulates the breathing via the central nervous system. But we don't like doing that, and in fact we can't do it for more than a few weeks. So let's hope this was a one-off with this little one.'

Joanna accompanied him to the door, as she was supposed to do.

'All right now?' he asked her. 'See if you can't organise a cup of tea, hot and strong and sweet—tell Sister it's doctor's orders.' He patted her shoulder. 'You dealt with that well, Nurse.'

For a moment she watched him stride off down the corridor, his white coat flying, and she thought, absurdly, can that be the same man who makes me dislike him so much, out of the hospital?

It was really quite strange, she decided a little later, when she was having tea, that two people who rubbed each other the wrong way so much—and there was no doubt that Rob disliked her just as much as she disliked him—in their personal lives, could work so well together, and could actually, she admitted with some reluctance, have quite a lot in common. Dr Jekyll and Mr Hyde, she thought—and there couldn't be a more professional and considerate and thoughtful man than Dr Rob Jekyll. While as for the arrogant Mr Hyde she knew outside the hospital—the less she thought about him, the better!

By tacit agreement, she and Cathy didn't talk about Rob. Cathy, quiet and gentle as she was, could dig her heels in, Joanna was sure, if she was pushed. At the moment Cathy seemed determined to regard Rob as a friend—or to say that she did. Joanna didn't want to risk criticising Rob, or attempting to point out to Cathy the many and varied reasons why Joanna felt he wasn't the sort of 'friend' Cathy should have, because she had the certainty that all Cathy's loyalty, misplaced or not, might rise to the surface and push the friendship into becoming something more.

What she could do, she decided, was to try, as unobtrusively as possible, to keep Cathy occupied in some of the time she might otherwise have spent with Rob Martin. This wasn't too difficult, with Colin working long hours, and Joanna and Cathy would often spend their free time together. Sometimes, even when Colin was free, Joanna would ask him if he minded if Cathy came along with them. He was polite, but not overly enthusiastic at first, and Cathy herself was most unwilling to come out with them, but after Joanna had spoken nicely to Colin, and assured Cathy that she and Colin liked having her with them, the threesome became if not a regular thing, at least accepted occasionally—and each occasion, Joanna told herself with satisfaction, meant a few hours that Cathy was kept out of the company of Rob Martin!

And it was nice, she thought more and more, to see how well Colin and Cathy got on together. They were both quiet people, really, and neither found it too easy to make new friends, but somehow, with Joanna to help things along, they came quite quickly to an easy and undemanding relationship.

'But you and Colin must have some time to yourselves, Joanna,' Cathy would insist, from time to time. 'It's not fair for you always to have me.'

'We don't, though,' Joanna would point out. 'Last night Colin and I had a lovely evening—we had dinner, and we walked along beside the sea, and it was so nice.'

She knew, in her honest and realistic moments, that things couldn't go on indefinitely like this. Sometimes she found Colin's eyes resting thoughtfully on her, and she knew she couldn't expect him to accept this situation for much longer. Not that she herself intended it to go on, she reminded herself from time to time. Just as she had said to Colin, all she really needed was a little time. After all, they had been apart for that year, it was only reasonable that they needed time to get used to being together again.

In some ways it was unfortunate that Colin's job was extremely demanding, and that he did have very little free time. Weekends were particularly difficult, when Joanna too was often on duty, and when they both happened to have a Saturday off Colin suggested that they should go to the beach early.

'I know it's autumn, but the weather is nicer than when it's too hot—and it does keep the real heat-lovers away. Do you remember how we used to go to the beach early and take a breakfast picnic, Joanna?' he said. 'Let's do that—we'll just pick up a couple of rolls at Wayne's, take apples, and a flask of coffee.'

'That would be lovely,' Joanna agreed, and the thought of the beach in the early morning was very tempting, after a demanding week in the Intensive Care Unit, where even the air, she sometimes thought, was so sterile that it wasn't real. 'Should I ask Cathy if she's off?'

Colin's hesitation was so brief that she could almost persuade herself that she had imagined it.

'Of course, if you would like to,' he said. And then, his eyes meeting hers, 'But I'd rather be on our own, Joanna. I'm very fond of Cathy, and mostly I'm happy to have her with us, but the beach breakfast used to be a special thing for us.'

'Then I won't ask Cathy,' she replied quietly. But just for a moment she had a fleeting sense of panic at the thought of Colin and herself, just on their own, doing this special thing, as he had called it. And Colin hoping all the time that she was beginning to feel differently about their relationship. And for the first time, then, she had a sudden and disquieting realisation that although she looked on the time Cathy spent with her and Colin as time well spent away from Rob Martin, perhaps—perhaps she also looked on Cathy's presence as a buffer, as a protection against being alone with Colin.

And that, she thought with a sinking heart, is

something I've got to work through. I can't just dismiss the thought, I've got to be honest with myself.

It was a beautiful autumn morning when they reached the beach at Camps Bay. Dropping down from Kloof Nek towards the sea, blue and sparkling ahead of them, Joanna was all at once very happy. Happy to be here, with Colin, in this place they had always loved. Happy to have this feeling of getting right away from the hospital and the demanding work she loved so much. Happy to have the beach to themselves, on this morning in early autumn, with the sand clean and untouched as they walked along it, and found a rock to sit at, to have their picnic.

'Instant coffee, but it tastes like the best coffee in the world, here on the beach, doesn't it?' commented Colin, as they drank their mugs of steaming coffee. 'Coffee and rolls—our own continental breakfast, here on our own continent.'

Joanna set her mug down in the sand and looked at him.

'So you didn't feel America was your continent?' she asked him.

He shook his head. 'Great place, but not my place,' he said with certainty. 'I missed so much about Cape Town. Places, and people. Funny, I knew I would miss you, but I didn't expect to miss people in general, just—South African folks. Oh, speaking of folks, my folks think that would be a great idea if a crowd of us went up to Hermanus, maybe the next long weekend.' For a moment his hand covered hers. 'It would be perhaps an easier way for you to meet them, just at first, honey, instead of coming up with me on your own. Less—compromising, maybe.'

Unexpected tears, both at his thoughtfulness and his perspicacity, blurred her eyes for a moment.

'Colin, I—'

'It's all right,' he said, quite gently. And then, with an obvious but welcome change of subject, he said that now that he had had breakfast, he was going to lie down and digest it.

'Lazy!' Joanna teased him, with a wave of affection.

'Not at all,' he told her. 'I just feel like thinking, and I think best with my eyes closed! If you're in your usual energetic beach mood, you can have a walk for me as well—I'll be waiting here when you come back.'

Joanna rolled up the legs of her jeans and left her shoes lying beside him. He was almost asleep as she walked away across the deserted beach, and she remembered, with compunction, that he had said yesterday he would probably work late, so that he could take the day off. And with Colin, late really did mean late.

The sea on this side was always icy cold, even in the middle of summer, since this was the Atlantic Ocean, and when Joanna, giving in to an impulse that she could never resist, dipped her feet in, she felt as if she had lost all feeling below her ankles. She ran along the beach, then, fast, to bring back circulation to her icy-cold feet, and it was only when she turned to come back that she saw the dog running towards her. He was an Irish setter, and he ran easily and happily towards her, his red-gold coat gleaming in the early morning sunshine.

'Aren't you beautiful?' said Joanna, bending down to speak to him. 'But where did you come from?'

'He lives here—so do I,' Rob Martin said, beside

her. 'I did mention to you that I had a cottage in Camps Bay—that's it.'

The cottage was virtually on the beach, and of course, as she could see now, he and the dog had walked down while she was running.

'I had forgotten,' she replied shortly, and not entirely truthfully, for since she and Colin parked the car and walked down to the beach, she had been putting out of her mind the memory of Rob Martin telling her he had a cottage in Camps Bay.

'Rufus insists on his early beach walk whenever I can manage it,' Rob said now, and she realised, a little to her surprise, that he felt as awkward as she did, away from the hospital and their work. 'Are you on your own?'

'No, Colin is here too,' she told him. And then, between relief and something she preferred not to identify, 'Oh, here he is, he's come to meet me.'

The big dog bounded towards Colin as he walked towards them, and Joanna waved, then began walking back the way she had come. After a moment Rob joined her, his long stride catching up with her easily. The two men greeted each other, and Colin admired the big dog.

'Come and have coffee with me,' Rob suggested easily. 'My cottage is just there.'

Joanna wanted to refuse, but Colin had already accepted. Rob waited while they gathered their belongings, then they walked with him across the beach, and along the little road leading to his cottage.

'I'll put the coffee on,' said Rob, unlocking the front door. 'Wait, Rufus—visitors first, and especially lady visitors.' For a moment his dark blue eyes met

Joanna's. 'Rufus likes it when we have lady visitors,' he said blandly. 'Sit down—and make yourselves at home.'

It was a comfortable and casual room, uncluttered. Surprisingly, there was a piano, and Joanna had walked across to it, to examine the music lying open, when she saw the photograph. A girl, smiling into the camera, her fair hair blowing in the breeze.

Cathy.

And then, almost in the same moment, she saw that it wasn't, in fact, Cathy, but a girl very like her.

Colin had joined her, and when Rob came through from the kitchen he turned to him.

'I thought this was Cathy, just for a moment,' he said. 'Very like her. Who is she?'

Rob didn't look at Joanna as he replied to Colin's question.

'My sister Laura,' he said evenly. 'She—was killed in a car crash two years ago.'

And now, for a moment, his eyes met Joanna's.

'Yes,' he said, and his voice was low, 'Cathy is very like her. I suppose that's why I can talk to her about Laura.'

CHAPTER TEN

'I'm sorry, Rob,' Colin said quietly.

Joanna said nothing; she was too distressed. He had said that he looked on Cathy as a sister, and she hadn't believed him.

Rob had turned away and was looking out of the window, towards the sea.

'It's a long time, two years,' he said, and it was all too obvious that he didn't want to say any more about his sister. 'That coffee should be ready now.'

The three of them sat out on the stoep, and Joanna was glad to be able to be silent while the two young doctors talked. Rob asked Colin about the research he was working on, and Colin, a little reluctantly at first, and then with enthusiasm when he saw how interested Rob was, talked about the work he was doing on new drugs to treat Parkinson's Disease.

Joanna, with the dog Rufus resting his head on her knee, sat listening to them as they talked about the problems of balancing drug dosage, and the side effects of the drugs necessary to control the disease. And she thought of a fair-haired, laughing girl called Laura, a girl who had died in a car crash two years ago. A girl Cathy resembled—oh, not closely, but just a little. He must have been very fond of his sister, she thought painfully. He—might even have talked to me about her, if I'd been more understanding, when he tried to tell me that he looked on Cathy as a sister.

But later, away from Rob and the cottage in Camps Bay, and the picture of his sister Laura, she began to think that in fact her reaction had been right at the start. It was all very well for Rob to say he looked on Cathy as a sister, but that didn't make Cathy any less likely to fall in love with him, and to be hurt. And sometimes, when Joanna looked at the younger girl, she was concerned about her, for she would catch a fleeting glimpse of sadness in Cathy's blue eyes, a shadow that shouldn't have been there. A shadow that wouldn't have been there, she began to tell herself, if it hadn't been for Rob Martin.

She talked to Lynn about her concern for Cathy, and Lynn, coming down from cloud seven where she seemed to be most of the time, since she had met her Michael, agreed that perhaps Cathy wasn't entirely happy.

'But there isn't really anything you and I can do about it, Jo,' she pointed out realistically. 'We can't live Cathy's life for her, we can't stop her making mistakes. You know how I feel, anyway—I don't think Rob Martin is quite the big bad wolf you think he is, and I don't think it would give him pleasure to make Cathy unhappy.'

Joanna couldn't agree.

'Cathy is too gentle, too sensitive, to handle a man like him,' she said stubbornly.

Lynn shrugged.

'In that case, all we can do is stand by with shoulders at the ready when she needs them.' She hesitated, but only for a moment, before going on. 'Jo, what about you and Colin? He's been back over six

weeks now—how come you're not getting engaged?
It's not because he doesn't want to.'

They had been friends for so long that Joanna
couldn't be anything but truthful. She hadn't said
anything to Lynn about her doubts, before this, partly
because of a feeling of disloyalty to Colin, and partly
because Lynn herself was so involved with Michael,
and so happy that Joanna felt bad about intruding her
own problems. But now that Lynn had spoken about
it, she was glad.

'Colin does want us to get engaged,' she replied
slowly. 'I—I just feel I need time to get accustomed to
him being back again.'

Lynn sat down at the kitchen table beside her, and
passed a mug of coffee across to Joanna.

'And it worries you, that you feel that way,' she
said.

Joanna nodded.

'I shouldn't have any doubts,' she admitted. 'And it
isn't that I don't think the world of Colin, I do, it's
just—'

It's just that I don't think I love him enough to
spend the rest of my life with him.

As clearly as if she had said it aloud, the thought
was there, for the first time spelled out.

'In fairness to Colin, you've got to sort yourself out,
you know,' Lynn said gently.

'I know that,' Joanna agreed. And then, with difficulty, 'I think I know what I have to do, it's just a
question of finding the right time.'

'Ducky, there never is a right time for this sort of
thing,' Lynn replied. 'But now that you're on night
duty, maybe you should let the whole thing ride for a

bit—I don't think anyone should make important decisions while they're on night duty! Concentrate on sleeping as much as you can, and working up your quota of babies! That's the one good thing about night duty.'

'I know,' said Joanna. 'I've already had three more deliveries.'

She was doing her spell of night duty up at the big hospital, and for part of the time she would be ready to go out with the Flying Doctor Squad, in the ambulance which the district units sent for, when they had an emergency. She was looking forward to this, but hoping, too, that she would have some time to build up her actual experience, before she was out in the ambulance.

But with each delivery she felt more and more confident, although she was sure she would never lose that sense of wonder as she held a newly-born baby up and then saw the mother take her baby in her arms for the first time.

She had been on night duty for just over a week when her first call to go out on the Flying Doctor service came through.

'Off you go, Nurse Winter,' the Sister in charge told her. 'Doctor is waiting in the ambulance—there's a forceps delivery out at the Hanover Park unit, the patient will be brought back here if possible; if there isn't time Doctor will deliver there.'

Joanna, her cloak wrapped around her against the chill of a night in early winter, hurried along the passage to the waiting ambulance.

'Hurry up, Nurse,' the waiting doctor told her, his back to her as he checked the two Resuscitation boxes, Infant and Maternal. 'Ready? All right, Tom, we can go.'

Joanna, from the moment he spoke, had had time to recover from the shock he obviously felt when he turned round.

'Oh, it's you,' said Rob. 'I didn't know you were on night duty.'

Joanna could have replied that she hadn't known he was, either, but of course a student midwife didn't speak like that to one of the registrars, so she remained silent.

'Two of the housemen are down with 'flu—I'm relieving,' Rob said curtly.

As they drove through the suburbs of the sleeping city, Joanna thought he wasn't going to say anything more. But when he did speak, he had obviously done as both he and she had on many occasions, and completely separated his working self from his private self.

'Have you seen a forceps delivery, Nurse?' he asked her.

'No, I haven't,' Joanna replied. And then, when he seemed to be waiting, 'I know the different reasons for applying forceps.'

She thought from his voice that he might be smiling, but in the dimly-lit ambulance it was difficult to tell.

'Right, tell me,' he said.

'Forceps are applied in the second stage only,' Joanna recited. 'Their use is indicated when there is delay in the second stage due to hypotonic uterine action, minor degrees of outlet contraction, deep transverse arrest, and persistent occipito-posterior position. Which is this case, Dr Martin?'

'Deep transverse arrest,' he told her. 'That head just isn't moving, apparently. You know, I'm sure, that we use forceps too when the mother is suffering from a serious degree of cardiac disease, or advanced pulmonary tuberculosis.' He peered out into the darkness. 'Almost there. You'll be on district here, at some stage.'

The ambulance pulled up outside the small obstetrical unit where mothers came in, had their babies, and went home quickly, if there were no complications. If there were, the Flying Squad was called in.

The Night Sister in charge was waiting for them, and after a quick report she took them through to the patient. Joanna watched as Rob did his examination, quickly, professionally, but with a warmth and an assurance that she could see helped the distressed and frightened young woman.

'I think we'll deliver your baby right away, Mrs Crawford,' he said easily, as he straightened up. 'Then we'll take the two of you through to the hospital and keep you there for a day or two. Nurse Winter, I'm going to use the Kielland's forceps.'

As he and Joanna scrubbed up, he told her, his voice low, that this was what he was using because of the need to rotate the baby's head as he delivered.

'This is going to be a fairly straightforward delivery,' he said, 'but I've asked Sister to ring through and have the paediatrician at the hospital to check the baby when we get back.'

Joanna was glad of the experience of the night Sister from the unit, as they checked, together, the equipment necessary, in case the baby was asphyxiated, as well as the requirements for catheterisation, episiotomy, and sutures.

And once more, as she watched Rob Martin in operation, she could have nothing but admiration for his professional ability. And more than that, she had to admit, when the baby was safely delivered, and he was supervising as she and Sister prepared mother and baby for the ambulance journey. He could always, as a doctor, go beyond the undoubted skill so necessary for any doctor, and somehow make real and human contact with his patients.

'He's a fine healthy boy,' he told the young mother reassuringly. 'Thanks to Sister getting in touch with us right away, he hardly even knows there was any hold-up. We'll have him checked and double-checked, to make sure, as soon as we reach the hospital. And Sister will get a message to your husband—he's a fisherman, you said?' He patted the baby, now securely in a small travelling cot. 'You're the one with a big catch tonight!'

The journey back was quiet, but with the drowsy young mother and the sleeping baby in the ambulance with them there was a warm and a happy feeling, Joanna thought—then told herself she was being fanciful.

'I always like that feeling of coming back here, with a happy mother and baby, both of them safe,' Rob said to her, when both mother and baby had been taken into the ward.

'I was thinking the same, as we came back,' she admitted, with an unaccountable lift in her heart.

She had two more journeys with Rob during that week, once when they were sent for to bring in a mother haemorrhaging badly after giving birth, and the next time, to bring a premature baby in to the Intensive Care Unit. Joanna was glad of her experience with premature babies, as she helped Rob to set up a drip and put the baby in a portable incubator, and kept a constant check that the baby's condition was stable.

'The night life of Cape Town, Joanna,' he said ruefully, as he left her back at the hospital. ''Bye!'

How very unprofessional of him, she thought, with a ridiculous thud of her heart, not to call me Nurse. Unprofessional—but nice, was the thought that she immediately crushed. Because this, she reminded herself severely, was Dr Jekyll—she mustn't forget Mr Hyde.

And she had a sobering reminder, just the next day, of the other side of this man, this doctor she had recently had to remind herself was the same arrogant and high-handed man who thought he was God's gift to young nurses.

She woke earlier than usual during her daytime sleep—the day which was her night, at the moment—and still half asleep, came through to the kitchen to make herself some coffee, and then perhaps go back and try for some more sleep.

Cathy was in the kitchen, alone, and she was sitting at the table, with her face buried in her hands, crying. For a moment Joanna wondered whether she should tiptoe out and pretend she hadn't seen or heard, but just as she decided that she couldn't do that, Cathy looked up and saw her.

'Joanna, I thought you were asleep,' she said shakily.

Acting purely on instinct, Joanna said nothing, but put her arms around the younger girl and held her tightly. For a moment Cathy tried to control her tears, then she gave in and clung to Joanna as she wept. There was little Joanna could do beyond murmuring Cathy's name, and just holding her. And slowly, as Cathy's sobs died away, Joanna found that she was no longer in any danger of forgetting the sort of man Rob Martin was. So he hadn't ever made any girl cry, had he! she thought indignantly, remembering what Lynn had said. So it had always been fun, good clean fun? It certainly didn't look too much like fun now, for Cathy.

When Cathy had stopped crying, Joanna handed her the box of tissues, wordlessly, and Cathy, with a watery smile, thanked her.

'I'll make some tea,' Joanna told her. 'Go and give your face a splash.'

When Cathy came back, she poured two mugs of tea. She knew she couldn't just leave things, she had to say something, but she waited until half of the mug of tea was gone.

'Cathy,' she said then, gently, 'he isn't worth it, you know.'

Cathy's blue eyes, washed with tears, were clear now.

'I can't agree with you,' she said, not stubbornly but firmly. 'I think he is worth it. I'll be all right now, Joanna, really. Thank you for being there.'

'I hate to see you unhappy,' Joanna told her, more fiercely than she had intended to. 'And for a man like Rob Martin.'

For a moment Cathy looked away, then her eyes met Joanna's.

'I wasn't crying because of Rob, Joanna,' she said quietly.

There was, of course, nothing Joanna could say to that. If Cathy's pride stopped her from admitting it, she certainly wasn't going to push. And she certainly wasn't going to say that she had known, right from the start, that nothing but unhappiness could come from falling for a man like Rob Martin.

CHAPTER ELEVEN

IF Joanna could have found a way to get out of the proposed weekend at Hermanus she would have been only too glad. But it was all arranged, and Colin's parents were expecting the group of young people, and very much looking forward to having them, Colin said.

Of the eight who were to make up the party, only Lynn's Michael, and Susan, the wife of Colin's colleague Lewis, were non-medical people, and the others had all, with considerable trouble, managed to switch and rearrange off-duty times so that they could leave on Friday evening and have the whole weekend.

The only thing Joanna promised herself was that she would take good care not to spend any more time than she had to in Rob Martin's company. Or anywhere near him, she told herself fiercely, remembering Cathy's tears. She and Colin drove up with Lewis and Susan, leaving the other four to come together.

She hadn't, she realised with shame, asked Colin much about his parents' move to Hermanus, and since they had lived in Durban before, this was her first meeting with them. As they drove through the little seaside town of Hermanus, she admitted to herself that she was just a little on edge about this meeting, for she knew that Colin would have told his parents a great deal about her—possibly told them, even, that they were planning to get engaged after his return from America.

But to her relief, Colin's parents greeted her warmly and kindly, but without making any difference between her and the rest of the group. The second car arrived soon after they did, and the eight young people sat on the stoep drinking coffee, talking to Colin's parents, and admiring the thatched house that looked out to sea.

'The cliff walk goes right along,' Colin's mother told them. 'It's a fine easy walk for old folk like us.'

Joanna loved Mrs Cameron's soft Scottish voice, and her smiling blue eyes, and as she sat telling her hostess about her own family in Johannesburg, and how much she missed them, she couldn't help wishing that she had been able to feel differently about a future for herself and Colin.

The next morning, when they set off to walk in the Fernkloof Nature Reserve, she had decided that as soon as possible she was going to talk to Colin. She had a feeling that he wouldn't be entirely taken by surprise, for sometimes she found him looking at her, thoughtfully, steadily, and disturbingly. Oh, they had talked sensibly about the possibility of either of them feeling differently, after the year apart, but that didn't make it any easier, now that he had actually asked her to marry him, now that he had shown her that he felt the same.

But I'm not the only girl in the world, Joanna told herself, using the stout stick provided for the steep parts of the walk, and Colin deserves better than this!

'You look very fierce, Joanna,' Rob Martin remarked, dropping into step beside her. 'Is it the result of night duty, or are you naturally fierce?'

There was laughter in his voice and a warm teasing in his eyes, but the memory of Cathy in tears, and denying that Rob was the cause of her tears, helped Joanna to resist the treacherous response that this man's nearness evoked in her.

'I'm naturally fierce,' she told him, her voice cool. 'And night duty I can take in my stride, thanks.'

She hoped he realised all that she meant when she said that—a refusal to allow any intimacy and closeness that had arisen between them when they were working together in the Flying Squad to make any difference to the way she felt about him.

For a moment his dark blue eyes held hers, then the warmth in his faded, and with an almost imperceptible shrug he stood back on the narrow path and allowed her to move on to catch up with Lynn and Michael, just ahead.

The view from the top was magnificent, with the whole of the bay, and the little fishing town, with its old harbour and its new harbour, spread out below them. Mrs Cameron had helped them to spread fresh rolls to bring with them, and these, with apples, and coffee, had been well worth the effort to carry up, everyone agreed.

'We were lucky to get such a lovely day,' said Joanna, uncomfortable suddenly as a long glance from Rob reminded her just how short her shorts were. 'And in June, too.'

'Almost midwinter,' Colin agreed. 'I'm told that Hermanus, like the rest of the Cape, can be pretty cold and wet in winter—but if you get the odd day like this in between, I reckon you can survive the rest.' He stood up. 'Cathy, you know that *disa* my father was telling you about last night? I think I could find it—anyone else want to have a look?'

No one else was energetic enough, with the thought of the long walk down again, and Colin and Cathy went off towards the waterfall. Joanna lay on her back, looking up at the seagulls wheeling in the blue of the sky, listening drowsily to the voices around her. Michael's, with the delightful Irish lilt, Susan's American drawl, the other South African voices. And Rob's voice, warm and laughing as he talked to Lynn.

They had a *braai* that night, with the men doing the cooking of the chops, steak and sausages, while the girls helped Mrs Cameron with rolls and salads.

'Och, it's a grand South African custom,' Colin's mother commented. 'I just feel you can keep your Women's Lib, when you have the chance to get the men to feel that they're the only ones who can make a good job of cooking the meat at a *braai*!'

Joanna looked up from the tomatoes she was slicing.

'I just don't like any man to feel he can do something better than I can,' she replied.

'Come now, Joanna,' chided Mrs Cameron, smiling, 'you have to reach the stage I have, where you know fine you can do it better—but you're happy enough to leave them to it! What do you think, Cathy?'

Cathy finished washing the lettuce, and smiled.

'I'm old-fashioned, Mrs Cameron,' she confessed. 'I still think there are some things women do better, and some things men do better. And I'm happy to have it that way.'

'Nothing wrong with being old-fashioned, lass,' Colin's mother agreed. 'Now, we'd better see how these experts out there are doing.'

The smell of the sizzling meat was tempting, and soon the group of people were sitting on the stoep, with their plates of meat and salad, and glasses of wine or beer. Joanna, sitting near Lynn and Michael, saw them exchange a glance and a murmured word, then Michael stood up.

'Sure and I don't know whether I should be waiting to say this, but I can't be keeping it to myself any longer—I just have to tell you all right now.' He took Lynn's hand and drew her to her feet too. 'We've just got engaged, Lynn and me,' he said proudly, looking down into Lynn's radiant face. 'And it's an invitation to the wedding you'll all be getting, just as soon as we can set the date.'

There was laughter and congratulations, and teasing and kissing, and amid all the happiness there was only one moment that distressed Joanna. Colin, turning from kissing Lynn and congratulating Michael, stood close to Joanna for a moment, his eyes holding hers.

This could have been us, he was saying silently, she knew.

And she wondered if he realised that she was replying, but I don't want it to be us.

She turned away, then, ill at ease, and found Rob standing at the back of the group watching them, unsmiling. Or so she thought, for a moment later, so quickly that she wondered if she had imagined the brooding expression on his face, he had moved forward to take his turn at talking to the newly-engaged couple.

That night, although she was tired with the fresh air and the unaccustomed exercise, she had difficulty sleeping, and she was glad when it was morning and she could pull on jeans and a sweater and tiptoe out of the house and across the rough grass to the cliff path. But when she turned the corner, Rob was standing there, his hair blowing in the sea breeze, his turtleneck sweater the same dark blue as his eyes.

'I've just been for a walk,' he told her, a little warily. 'I was wishing I had Rufus with me, he would love this.'

'Who looks after him when you're away like this?' Joanna asked politely, wary herself.

'The girl next door feeds him and takes him out—she's very fond of him,' said Rob.

'I can imagine,' Joanna returned, more tartly than she had meant to. But having said that much, she might as well go on, she decided, and she laughed, lightly, brightly. 'I'm sure you'll always find a girl next door ready to look after your dog when you need her to!'

She hadn't thought the blue of his eyes could become so icy.

'This girl,' he said, very coolly, 'is a schoolgirl of eleven. I play squash with her father. Sorry about that, Joanna—you do like to think the very worst of me, don't you?'

Joanna turned away.

'I'm going for a walk,' she said.

'Better not be long,' he returned. 'Didn't we all

decide to start early for the trip to Gansbaai?'

Joanna had momentarily forgotten the plan, in her agitation at meeting him here on the cliffs.

'I'll have a short walk,' she said perversely, and walked off briskly along the cliff path to the next little headland, where she turned and walked even more briskly back.

He was still standing where she had left him.

'Enjoy your walk?' he asked her pleasantly.

'Very much, thanks,' Joanna told him, not entirely truthfully, for she hadn't been in the best of moods to enjoy the cliffs and the sea. Without waiting for him, she walked up the path and across to the house, where she was glad to find Colin's mother in the kitchen, delighted to have help in making breakfast for her hungry guests.

'Colin had a great idea,' Lynn told her as they washed the breakfast dishes. 'We've booked lunch for all of us at a little hotel called De Kelders, just before Gansbaai. Colin's parents were there a few weeks ago, and you get one of these super Sunday country hotel lunches. But we're going right now, because we want to see the caves.'

Somehow, the arrangement of people had been changed, and Joanna found that it was Rob and Cathy who were with Colin and her. Just as well, she found herself thinking, that the two men seemed to have plenty to talk about, because neither she nor Cathy was very talkative.

They parked the two cars outside the hotel and bought tickets for the mineral water swimming bath, right down in the cliffs, at sea level. One after the other they made their way down the steep flight of steps and into the rough-hewn opening in the cliff face at the bottom.

Joanna didn't know what she expected to see, but it certainly wasn't the reasonably well lit, low-roofed cave, with natural pools of water, deep enough to swim in, on each side. She put her fingers in the water and found it wasn't as cold as she had expected.

'What an incredible place,' she remarked. 'The lights are obviously modern, but it has such an old feeling about it.

Colin, beside her, nodded.

'Lady Anne Barnard visited it in 1798,' he told her. 'No lights then, of course, and she called it the darkest cave in Africa.'

Thank goodness for the lights, Joanna thought, and even with the lights she began to feel less and less happy. She never had liked enclosed spaces, and somehow, the low roof of the cave seemed to press down on her. In spite of the warmth of the cave, she felt her forehead become cold and damp, and she tried unobtrusively to wipe it.

'Look, there's a passage over here!' Lynn called, from the other side, and everyone moved towards her. Everyone except Joanna. For something had just brushed against her cheek, and she was frozen with the realisation that it was a bat. A bat—as well as an oppressive and claustrophobic cave! Desperately she wanted to move, to join the others, even, ashamed as she would have been to do it, to scream. But she couldn't move, and her throat was frozen with something worse than mere fright.

And then a hand closed on hers, large and warm and infinitely reassuring.

'It's all right,' Rob Martin told her, his voice low. 'Hang on to me.'

He called across to the others then.

'Personally, I can't stand bats—I'll wait outside while you investigate. Coming with me, Joanna? Good.'

She didn't know, afterwards, how he managed to get her moving, but somehow he did, his hand holding hers tightly all the time, even when they were outside the cave and standing beside the sea, in the fresh air.

Joanna closed her eyes and felt herself sway lightly, before Rob's hands closed firmly on her shoulders.

'You're not going to faint now,' he told her. 'Just keep walking, and breathe deeply.'

Obediently, because her legs still felt like jelly, and so did her brain, she did as he told her, and followed him round into a small bay.

'Now you can sit down,' he said, and half pushed her down beside a rock. Joanna leaned back against it, and she kept her eyes closed until she was certain she felt better. When she opened them Rob was looking at her with some concern.

'Thank you,' she said awkwardly. 'I—I just went to pieces.'

'I know, I saw that,' he replied.

He was still looking at her, and she was unable to look away. She never knew, afterwards, which of them moved first, all she knew was that she was in his arms, and his lips were hard on hers, and in spite of all that she knew and disliked about this man, she wanted this kiss to go on for ever. She put her hands in his thick fair hair, holding him more closely, and now she could feel his heart thudding. Or was it her heart? She didn't know, and it didn't matter.

And then, abruptly, he drew back from her.

'I'm sorry,' he said, and the cold formality of his voice was like a splash of cold water, reminding her—reminding her of all that his kiss had made her forget. 'I really do make a habit of taking advantage of you, don't I?'

Warm colour flooded Joanna's face, because he must know as well as she did the effect he had on her. Purely physical, purely chemistry, but a devastating, disturbing effect, all the same.

'Don't worry about it,' she returned, and somehow she managed to keep her voice steady, and as cool as his had been. 'I certainly won't give it another thought!'

She knew, as she said it, how completely untruthful that was, but she was determined that she would never let this man know what his touch could do to her.

CHAPTER TWELVE

THEY reached the entrance to the cave and the underground swimming bath just as the others came out. Neither Rob nor Joanna had said another word—Joanna because she was too shaken by Rob's kiss, and her own reaction to it, to speak, and Rob, she presumed, because he didn't feel like speaking.

'I'm going back to swim there in summer,' announced Lynn. 'I'm not mad about bats, either, Rob, but I'd just love to say I'd swum where Lady Anne Barnard swam!'

Their lunch in the hotel near the caves, was extremely good, but Joanna felt she couldn't do justice to it. Half her mind—and half her appetite, she thought ruefully, looking at the crisp golden roast potatoes—seemed to be elsewhere. She found she couldn't look at Rob without a revealing warmth creeping into her face, and she was furious with herself for behaving like a schoolgirl and giving in to his undoubted magnetism as he obviously expected every girl to.

Fortunately he seemed as keen to avoid her as she was to avoid him, and when they all went for a walk after lunch he was far ahead, with Cathy, talking to her, his head bent towards her.

Inevitably, the group had split into couples. A little behind Cathy and Rob, Lynn and Michael walked slowly, hand in hand. Lewis and Susan were sitting on the beach, and Colin and Joanna were together.

'I do like your parents, Colin,' Joanna said sincerely. 'It makes me realise how much I miss my own family, being with your mother and father. They seem to have settled nicely here.'

'Yes, they're very happy,' he agreed. 'I was worried about them when I heard Dad was taking early retirement because of this heart condition, and making the move from Durban to Hermanus, but they seem to feel very much at home here, and I can see he's so much better.'

They walked along in silence for a while, and Joanna, coming out of her own abstraction, could see now that he was unusually quiet and thoughtful. She wasn't too surprised when he turned to her.

'Joanna,' he said quietly, 'I think we should have a talk—about us.'

It was what she had been wanting to do, and meaning to do, and yet all at once, she knew she couldn't handle it right now. I feel too fragile emotionally, she thought, trying to laugh herself out of this, but it was no good. Not here, not now—when her whole body still ached with the memory of her response to the kiss of a man she disliked so much.

'I know, Colin,' she said quickly, 'but—but please, let's leave it for now. Tonight—tomorrow—but not right now.'

'I wanted to get things clear—I've been doing some thinking, and I'm—' he began.

I'll cry if I have to go into an emotional scene now, Joanna realised, dismayed.

'Please, Colin, not now,' she begged unsteadily,

and put one hand on his arm and tried to smile.
'Later.'

She thought he was going to insist, but after a
moment he smiled too, although the smile didn't
reach his eyes, and shrugged.

'All right,' he replied, his voice low.

Michael and Lynn were coming towards them now,
and there was no opportunity, in any case, to say any
more. They made their way back to the hotel and the
cars, and drove back round the bay to Hermanus and
Colin's parents' home, where Colin's mother had tea
and newly-made scones ready.

Cathy was very quiet, Joanna suddenly noticed,
and she looked distressed. Once or twice, she didn't
answer when someone spoke to her, and when she
finally got up and went out of the room, Joanna
followed her, finding her in the bedroom the girls had
shared.

'If that man has been upsetting you again, Cathy,'
she said, going across to the younger girl, who was
standing looking out the window, 'I'll—'

Cathy turned to her, and Joanna, shocked, saw that
her face was grey.

'I don't feel very well, Joanna,' she said, and
Joanna saw that her forehead was damp. 'Actually, I
haven't felt too well all the weekend, but I didn't
want to say. I've got this awful pain—I thought it
might be indigestion or something, but it's getting
worse.'

Joanna took Cathy's wrist in hers, swiftly, professionally, fighting down the rising panic at the way
Cathy looked. Pulse racing—and already in shock,
with her skin like that.

'Lie down, Cathy,' she said, keeping her voice steady. 'I think we'd better get someone in to have a look at you—no, I'm not fussing, just taking advantage of all these medics around.'

She pulled the duvet around the younger girl and hurried back through. Afterwards, she was to remember that without any conscious thought or any decision, she turned to Rob.

'Cathy's ill,' she said to him. 'I mean really ill. Please come and have a look at her.'

He followed her out of the room, without question, and she saw that one glance at Cathy told him that she hadn't exaggerated. He bent over the girl on the bed and examined her, swiftly, professionally, asking a few questions which Cathy now seemed barely able to answer.

'I'm going to give you something to make you more comfortable, Cathy,' he said quietly. 'And I'm afraid we're going to have to get you to hospital.' He turned to Joanna. 'You probably suspected appendicitis, Joanna, and that's what it is.'

Thank goodness a doctor even off duty carries his medical case with him, Joanna thought, as she watched Rob give Cathy an injection.

'This will work pretty quickly,' he told the girl on the bed, his voice reassuring. 'We'll just make some arrangements about getting you away.'

He closed the bedroom door when he and Joanna were out, and looked down at her, and now the confidence and the reassurance had gone.

'Acute,' he said quietly, 'and if it hasn't already ruptured, it's close to it. I'm afraid we'll be talking about peritonitis now.'

He pushed open the door to the stoep, where the others were, and strode in.

'We need to get Cathy to hospital, stat,' he said crisply. 'Acute appendicitis, if not ruptured now, it will soon. Colin—ambulance?'

Colin had gone white with shock, but his reactions, too, were quick. He turned to his father.

'Jan van Zyl?' he said, and his father nodded.

'I'll ring him,' he said, hurrying out of the room.

'Farmer friend of Dad's, with his own plane,' Colin explained. 'As soon as Dad gets hold of him, I'll ring the hospital and get them to have an ambulance waiting at the airport. We can have her there in half an hour, if Jan is there.'

Joanna, not waiting to hear what was to happen, went back to sit with Cathy, already drowsy under the injection Rob had given her. It seemed an eternity before Colin came in.

'We've put the back of the station-wagon flat,' he said, his eyes on the now unconscious girl. 'I'll carry her out. Give me that blanket, Joanna.'

Gently they wrapped the blanket around Cathy, and Colin carried her carefully out to the waiting car. Rob was already at the wheel, and Colin and Joanna sat in the back, keeping Cathy's slight figure steady as Rob drove, fast, out of the small town and towards the farm and the waiting plane.

The farmer was already there, and the engine of the small plane roaring.

'They'll have an ambulance waiting in Cape Town, and the theatre will be ready,' said Colin. 'Have you got clearance, Jan?'

'Everything's in order,' the big farmer said. 'But I

can only take one of you, as well as the girl.'

Joanna, hearing this, assumed that Rob would go with Cathy, but there was one glance between the two men, and Colin climbed into the plane, waiting for Rob and Joanna to lift Cathy up to him.

Everything had happened so quickly that in no time at all the small plane had taken off, and Rob and Joanna were heading back towards Hermanus. Rob said nothing, and she was grateful for that, until they reached Colin's home.

'You need a cup of tea, strong and sweet,' he said to her brusquely.

'I'm a nurse,' she reminded him, perversely annoyed because he had seen how upset and shaken she was. 'I'm used to people being ill.'

For a moment his hand covered hers, as warm and as comforting as it had been in the cave. And then, as if regretting his action, he took it away.

'It's different when it happens to someone you're fond of,' he said, surprisingly gently. 'And you are fond of Cathy, aren't you?'

'Yes—yes, I am,' Joanna replied shakily, unnerved by his concern.

He hesitated.

'Joanna—' he began, then stopped, as Colin's mother hurried out to them.

'Did you get the poor wee lass away?' she asked. 'Now the other four have gone—Lynn said she'd get some of Cathy's things up to the hospital and leave whichever two of you came back now to drive Colin's car back. I've got a thermos filled for you, and some biscuits ready, because you'll not be wanting to put off any time.'

There wasn't even time for Joanna to feel dismayed at the thought of the drive back to Cape Town alone with Rob, and in fact, there was no room for anything but concern for Cathy. Within ten minutes they were driving off, Joanna promising to let Mrs Cameron know how Cathy was.

'Thank heavens for the new road,' Rob said tersely, as they streaked across the smooth straight national road heading for Cape Town. 'And thank heavens for Colin's taste in fast cars—if we meet a traffic cop, I'm prepared to argue our case with him!'

He glanced at her.

'Sleep if you want to,' he told her. 'You look exhausted.'

Joanna felt exhausted, but anxiety about Cathy kept her from giving in to her weariness.

'Do you think they'll get it out before it ruptures?' she asked, not too steadily.

'Joanna, I can't tell,' Rob replied honestly. 'You know that as well as I do, I'm sure.'

'And I know, too, how serious peritonitis can be, even in this day and age,' she said bleakly.

They stopped for five minutes, at the top of the pass leading down to Gordon's Bay and Somerset West, to drink the coffee from the flask. It was worth the brief stop, Joanna knew, for she could see that Rob needed even that short break.

'Straight to the hospital?' he asked her, and she nodded.

It was strange, being in the hospital and not in uniform, waiting, as so many times she had seen friends and relatives waiting, for news of Cathy.

'They're operating now,' said Colin, coming in,

white-faced. 'I'm pretty sure it had ruptured—she was in shock when we got her here.'

So many times during her training, Joanna thought, she had wheeled patients out of theatre after operations. She had always been concerned for them, and she had always taken the time to talk to the relatives, to reassure them whenever possible. But Rob was right, this was completely different. To see Cathy on the trolley, white and still, with a drip set up, made her forget any professional detachment that might have helped.

'They're taking her to intensive care,' Colin said quietly. 'They've loaded her with antibiotics, but they think the infection had spread pretty rapidly before they got in.'

He looked at Joanna.

'You're supposed to be on duty, remember,' he said, with an effort. 'I'll hang around here—I'll—let you know if there's any news. Lynn said to tell you she'd taken your uniform to the ward for you, and she'd tell Night Sister what had happened.'

There was nothing any of them could do for Cathy, and yet it was with reluctance that Joanna left that part of the hospital and made her way round the corner to the maternity block. Both Rob and Colin were waiting, and both, she thought as she changed into her uniform, were pretty concerned. Rob would be thinking of his sister Laura, and remembering.

It was a busy night on the ward, but she was glad there were no calls for the Flying Squad, for she wanted to be there, at the hospital, so that she could hear whatever news there was of Cathy. In the morning, as soon as she came off duty, she hurried round to

Main Block and up to the Intensive Care Room.

Both Rob and Colin were still there, drinking coffee.

'How is she?' Joanna asked breathlessly. 'Can I see her?'

Rob shook his head.

'You can look through the window, that's all they've let us do. She doesn't seem to be responding to the drugs, Joanna, and they're worried about not being able to control the infection. Here, have some of my coffee, you've been working all night.'

And you, she thought, have been awake too, and perhaps it's been easier for me, keeping occupied.

'You were on call,' she said to him, remembering this. 'Were you needed?'

He shook his head, and handed her the coffee cup.

'You both look pretty awful,' Joanna told them candidly. And then, with a tremendous effort, 'If—if you are allowed in to see Cathy, you'll give her the fright of her life, to see you looking like that!'

The two doctors looked at each other.

'She's right,' Rob admitted. 'I'm off to shower and shave—I'll keep in touch.'

'I'll do the same,' said Colin, when Rob had left them. 'I guess I might as well be in the lab.' He looked at her. 'Go home and get some sleep, Joanna, there's nothing any of us can do.'

Knowing he was right, but still reluctant, she gave in and went back to the flat. There was a note from Lynn, asking for news of Cathy, and Joanna phoned the hospital and persuaded the receptionist to put her through to the ward where Lynn was working.

'I'll go up when I come off duty,' said Lynn, when

Joanna had told her the little there was to tell. 'You've got to get some sleep, Jo, you're on duty again tonight. Have something to eat, and get off to bed. Maybe I'll have good news when I get there.'

Joanna didn't think she would be able to sleep, but by the time she finished the tea and toast she had made, waves of weariness were washing over her. She got into bed, and the next thing she knew was waking to hear her bedroom door opening softly, and then closing.

Lynn, back from the hospital, she realised, and she got up and hurried through, without thinking of pulling her dressing-gown over her brief and see-through pyjamas.

'Lynn, I'm awake!' she called, hurrying into the kitchen where she could hear the sound of the kettle boiling.

Lynn wasn't alone; Rob was with her. But Joanna had no more than one moment of dismay at her lack of clothes before she forgot everything else, at the sight of both their faces.

'Cathy?' she queried unsteadily.

'She's on the danger list,' Rob told her wearily. 'I phoned her parents, and they're coming right away. Michael is going to meet them at the airport.'

Lynn poured tea for all three of them, and Joanna saw that she had been crying.

'I'll go up to the hospital,' she said, drinking her tea quickly. 'I'm only on duty at seven, so I could stay there for a couple of hours.'

'I'll take you up,' offered Rob, finishing his own tea. 'Lynn, we'll let you know if there's—any news.'

And Joanna knew, numbly, that she hadn't imagined his momentary hesitation.

To her surprise, when they reached the Intensive Care Unit, Colin was in beside Cathy's bed. He hadn't seen them, and he was sitting looking at the girl in the bed.

'I thought they weren't allowing us in,' Joanna murmured to Rob, as they looked through the door.

'Pal of his in charge,' Rob told her. 'Max Johnson's nephew.'

'Colin looks worn out,' she said. 'I'll take over, I can sit there with Cathy, and he can go off and rest. I'll just tell the Sister in charge.'

Rob's hand on her shoulder stopped her.

'Wait a minute, Joanna,' he said. 'I—didn't want to have to say it, not like this, but Colin wants to be there, with Cathy, nothing will make him leave her.'

She looked at him, not understanding, bewildered by the unexpected compassion in his eyes.

'Are you blind, Joanna?' he demanded, suddenly angry. 'Can't you see that Colin is in love with her?'

CHAPTER THIRTEEN

COLIN—in love with Cathy?

'Come and have some coffee,' said Rob, and now all the anger had gone from his voice. 'We'll come back here in ten minutes. Just come now, Joanna.'

For once she was completely unable to argue with him, and she let herself be led along the corridor and into one of the small rooms used by the doctors on duty. There was no one else there, and Rob made her sit down on the couch.

'I'm going for some coffee,' he told her.

At the door he hesitated, then he turned and came back to her, and took both her hands in his.

'Don't look like that, Joanna,' he said roughly. 'Just start getting used to the idea.'

Yes, she thought, with unaccustomed obedience, when the door had closed behind him, I'll start getting used to the idea. Colin—in love with Cathy. Colin, and Cathy.

She thought of something, then. She remembered that Colin had wanted to talk to her, that moment in Hermanus, and she had stopped him, because she thought he wanted her to give him an answer—to say she would marry him. And instead he had wanted to tell her that he was in love with Cathy.

It's very funny, actually, she thought painfully. And then, with a stab—no, it isn't funny, nothing is funny, with Cathy lying there on the danger list, and

Colin sitting there with her, worrying about me as well. She stood up as Rob came back in, with two cups of steaming coffee.

'I've got to talk to Colin,' she told him urgently.

Swiftly he put down both cups, and caught her by the shoulders.

'Oh no,' he said firmly. 'You'll do no such thing. Colin has enough on his plate worrying about Cathy, without you laying into him.'

She could feel all the colour drain from her face.

'That—wasn't what I intended doing,' she said, not quite steadily. She could see that he didn't know whether to believe her or not. 'I just want to tell him it's all right,' she added, with difficulty.

Slowly the hostility left his face, and there was nothing but compassion left. And that unnerved her so much that she had to brush the back of her hand across her eyes.

'Don't cry, Joanna,' Rob said unevenly. 'For heaven's sake, don't cry. Look, sit down and drink this, and you'll feel better.'

He said nothing more until she had drunk half the cup of coffee.

'I didn't expect you to be hit so hard by it,' he said, then, his voice low.

Joanna tried to explain.

'I'm not hard hit, it's just—I'm having problems understanding. I mean, only a few weeks ago Colin asked me to marry him.' Afterwards she realised with some surprise that it had seemed quite natural for her to be talking so freely to this man she disliked so much.

'I know,' Rob replied, and she looked at him, even

more surprised. He coloured. 'Colin and I have become quite friendly, strange as that may seem to you,' he explained.

Joanna didn't feel like asking why, so she said nothing.

'He told me that when you wouldn't give him an answer then, when you wanted things to go on as they were, he took a long clear look at how things were between the two of you. And he began to think that perhaps it was nothing more than affection, and habit, keeping you together.' He looked embarrassed now. 'I don't like telling you this, Joanna, and it isn't really anything to do with me.'

Joanna put her empty coffee cup down on the table.

'Colin did try to tell me, I see that now,' she said, almost to herself. And she looked at Rob levelly. 'But none of this really matters, with Cathy so ill. Except—except that I'm glad I know, because I can tell Colin to stop worrying about me, and just think of Cathy.' She stood up. 'So I'm going along there now, to tell him that,' she said quietly.

He looked down at her, his blue eyes very dark.

'I'm sorry, Joanna,' he said.

'It's all right, Rob, really it is,' she told him, meaning it. She wanted, very much, for him to understand that this was completely true, that she wasn't heartbroken at losing Colin, that she was more than anything annoyed at herself for her lack of understanding. But it wouldn't be easy, and why should he care anyway? she asked herself.

There was no chance then for her to speak to Colin, because Cathy's parents had just arrived, and Joanna

waited while they went in, very quietly, to look at
Cathy. Her own eyes blurred when Cathy's mother
kissed the unconscious girl's forehead, gently,
lovingly.

Colin came out to the waiting-room with them, and
Joanna, her heart aching for him, saw that there were
shadows of exhaustion under his eyes.

'No change,' he said quietly, in answer to her
unspoken questions. 'Joanna, what about Cathy's
parents? They want to be near, and they should be
within reach of a telephone, but they're both tired,
I'm sure they could do with some rest before they
come back here.'

'Mrs Dawson won't want to leave Cathy,' Joanna
pointed out. 'But maybe they'll come back to the flat
with me, have a couple of hours' rest, and I could
bring them back when I come on duty.'

Cathy's mother, small and fair and very like Cathy,
wanted to stay as near her daughter as she would be
allowed to, but between Joanna and Colin and her
husband, she was persuaded to go back and have
some rest.

'I'll phone, if there's any change,' Colin promised.

Joanna took Cathy's parents back to the flat, and
made tea and toast for them, although Mrs Dawson
insisted she couldn't eat a bite. But when she had
finished one slice of toast, and a cup of tea, she
admitted that she felt better, and she and Joanna
pulled an extra mattress into Cathy's room so that she
and Cathy's father could both rest.

'I won't sleep,' she insisted unsteadily.

'You don't have to,' Joanna told her. 'Just lie
down—you do look tired, and that would worry

Cathy, when she—when she begins to feel better and sees you.'

And that, she told herself unhappily, wasn't entirely honest, giving the impression that they expected Cathy to begin improving any minute, but maybe, in the circumstances, it was not such a bad thing. She knew, from things Cathy had said, that her mother wasn't very strong, and anything that lessened the strain of this even a little was surely worth while.

There was no phone call, and Joanna, strained and weary herself, didn't know whether to think that was good or bad. When it was almost time for her to go on duty, she took more tea in for Cathy's parents, and told them she would take them back to the hospital.

'Lynn will be along some time,' she told them, 'and she could bring you back down—you'll sleep here, of course.'

Cathy's mother shook her head.

'No, dear,' she said quietly, determinedly, 'I'll be at the hospital, with Cathy.'

Joanna didn't try to make her change her mind, because she knew that her own mother would have done just the same.

Colin came to the Intensive Care door with her, when she had left Cathy's parents sitting beside their daughter.

'She just isn't responding to any of the drugs,' he said wearily, 'and they've given her a wide spectrum. I've seen this before, Joanna, with peritonitis.'

'We're not giving up hope, Colin,' Joanna told him firmly. 'Some of these drugs take some time to have any effect, you know that.' She looked up at the big clock on the wall. 'I'm sorry, Colin, but I'm on duty, I have to go.'

He looked down at her, and she saw that for the first time he was thinking of something beyond his concern for Cathy.

'Joanna,' he said, with obvious difficulty, 'I wanted to talk to you yesterday, but you said later. I know this isn't the time or the place, but you've got to know how I feel about Cathy.'

'I do know, Colin,' she replied quietly. 'It's all right, you know—I understand.'

Well, I'm trying to, she told herself honestly, as she hurried away from him and round to the Maternity Block. But the look of relief in his eyes had made it worth while saying it.

That night, surprisingly, was fairly quiet on the ward. Joanna delivered two babies, and was congratulating herself on another two for her quota, with everything quiet and peaceful, and only an hour to go before her night duty was over, when the mother of the first baby delivered suddenly haemorrhaged. Joanna, walking around the now darkened ward with her torch in her hand, heard, before she reached the bed, the shallow and irregular breathing.

Alarmed, she hurried over, and found the woman's pulse was racing rapidly and her skin was already cold and clammy. Working swiftly, Joanna applied pads and pressure, and rang the bell for the other night nurse.

'Send for the doctor in charge,' she said, without looking up. 'Tell him postpartum haemorrhage, rapid pulse, and falling blood pressure.'

She hadn't consciously wondered if it might be Rob

Martin on duty, but she was more than glad to find him beside her, taking charge, ordering a drip to be set up, and the foot of the bed to be elevated even further.

The day staff had come on duty before Rob and Joanna and the assistant nurse were satisfied that they had succeeded in stabilising the woman's condition.

'She'll do,' Rob said at last, wearily. 'You off duty now, Nurse?' Joanna nodded. 'Yes, we both are. I think I'll go right over and see how Cathy is. Have you—?'

He shook his head. 'Busy night,' he explained. 'Not your ward, but the others have had a few dramas. I'll wait for you.'

Hostilities are suspended, Joanna thought, as she drew her cloak around her, because of Cathy. And she was too weary to work out just how she felt about that.

Cathy's mother was asleep on a couch in the waiting-room, with a blanket over her.

'Don't get up,' Rob said quickly, when Mr Dawson would have stood up. 'Don't disturb your wife, I'm sure she needs the rest.'

Carefully, tenderly, Mr Dawson eased the weight of his wife's head on his arm. He, too, looked tired, Joanna saw. But surely—?

'She's improving,' he said quietly. 'The doctor was in half an hour ago, and he came right back to tell us that she's at last responding to the drugs. She isn't conscious yet, but we're here, waiting.'

Relief, combined with exhaustion, made Joanna realise, suddenly, that she had to sit down, and she did so, very quickly, just as Colin came into the room.

'They've taken her off the danger list,' he told them. 'No, don't wake her, Mr Dawson, we'll tell her later.' And then, levelly, 'You understand, her recovery is going to take some time, but she's going to be all right.'

He smiled, a tentative smile, unused in these last few days.

'I'm hungry,' he said, sounding surprised.

'I could believe that,' Rob replied, and he was smiling too. 'I bet you haven't eaten since we left Hermanus. Are you going to stay here, or have something to eat and then come back?'

Colin looked at his watch.

'They say she isn't likely to know much at all for the next hour, but I don't want to risk being away.' He looked at Joanna. 'Coming down to the canteen with me?' he asked her, a little awkwardly.

All Joanna wanted was to get home and go to bed and sleep for hours, now that she knew that Cathy was going to be all right. But she owed this to Colin, and she had to give him the time, right now.

'Yes, I'll come, Colin,' she replied, getting up and putting her cloak on again. For a moment Rob's eyes met hers, and there was a look of approval in his, that for some reason pleased her.

She sat waiting at the small table, while Colin collected bacon and eggs for himself, and a cup of coffee for her. And she thought of the many times she had sat like this before, waiting for Colin. Now that was finished and over.

Colin put the tray down on the table.

'I don't know what to say, Joanna,' he began slowly.

'I do,' she replied, because all at once she did. She sat up straight. 'It was good while it lasted, Colin— you and I. I think we'll always be friends, and I hope I'm right in that. You know how fond of Cathy I am—I've come to see, over these past few days, that she's the sister I've never had. I'd like to go on like that, Colin, and I don't see why we can't.'

She smiled.

'Don't let your bacon and eggs get cold, in your relief at being off the hook!' she told him. 'Eat first—talk later!'

He smiled. 'You always were a bit bossy for me,' he told her, and the gentle, tentative teasing warmed her heart. 'Cathy will do what I tell her!'

'I wouldn't be too sure of that,' Joanna warned him, her heart lightening.

He put his fork and knife down, and now he was serious again.

'It was always on the cards, of course, that we should change, in that time apart,' he said, as much to himself as to her. 'I just didn't expect it to happen, though, in spite of knowing that. And when I came back, and you obviously felt differently, I was only too glad, at first, to give you time. That night at the dance, when I asked you to marry me—this sounds awful, Joanna, but it was only when you wouldn't say yes right away that I realised that I was actually relieved! And—well, I got down to some clear thinking, and stopped deceiving myself, and began to admit that I was falling in love with Cathy.'

Joanna pushed his cup of coffee across the table to him, and he began to drink it, almost without noticing.

'At first I thought—nice girl, but a bit of a nuisance, the way she's always around. Then I began to get used to having her around, and—well, that day in Hermanus, that's what I wanted to say to you. I wanted us to call it a day, you and I, so that I could tell Cathy how I felt about her. And then she was ill.'

The memory of those terrible days was back in his eyes again, and Joanna felt a wave of affection for this man who would always have a special place in her heart. She leaned across the table and put her hand over his.

'It's all right, Colin,' she reminded him. 'Cathy's going to be all right.'

'Mind if I interrupt?' said Rob's voice, brusquely. For a moment his eyes met Joanna's, and the cool dislike in his shook her. 'I came to tell you, Colin, that Cathy's mother and father have just been in with her, and Cathy's mother says she opened her eyes and knew them. I should imagine you'd want to get right up there—unless you're too busy?'

The pointed insult in that escaped Colin entirely, as he rose from the table and hurried off. But it certainly didn't escape Joanna, and for one ridiculous moment, she found herself almost rushing into explanations of what Rob obviously thought was a tender scene.

'Find it difficult to let go, do you?' he said now, so rudely that Joanna heard herself gasp. But he didn't even wait to give her a chance to reply, for he turned and walked away, his head high, and—and arrogant as ever Joanna told herself furiously.

Not that it mattered in the slightest what Rob Martin thought of her, she reminded herself. It was just—annoying, that he seemed to have made up his mind that she was being something of a dog in the manger, about Colin.

And, she told herself bitterly as she too hurried out of the hospital, I doubt if dog is the word he would use, considering the way he looked at me just now!

In spite of the turmoil in her mind, she slept deeply for most of the rest of the day, waking up just in time to bath, have something to eat, and get ready to go on duty.

Thank goodness this spell of night duty is almost over, she thought, catching sight of her face in the hall mirror—much paler than usual, her eyes grey and shadowed, and even her hair, she thought, looking tired! She took five minutes to put some blusher on, and to brush her hair, before pinning it up ready for work. Still time, she thought, to look up and see how Cathy was doing. She wouldn't, surely, be allowed visitors yet, but at least any news would be right up to the minute.

But to her surprise, she was allowed to go in to see Cathy.

'Just for two minutes,' Sister Ripley warned her. 'You are Joanna, aren't you? Yes, I thought I remembered you from your training. She does seem to want to see you, but just very briefly.'

Joanna, trained nurse as she was, and experienced in seeing people who had been extremely ill, was still shaken at the translucent pallor of Cathy's face and the violet shadows around her eyes and her mouth.

'Two minutes, Sister told me,' she said softly as she sat down next to the bed. 'How do you feel?'

'Not very how at all,' Cathy admitted, and the tiny

attempt at a joke caught at Joanna's heart. 'But – oh, Joanna, Colin says you know, and—and—'

'And everything's fine,' Joanna told her firmly. 'Just hurry up and get well, and we can do all the talking you want.'

Cathy closed her eyes then, but her fingers were still holding Joanna's lightly. After a moment Joanna, catching sight of Sister's cap outside, gently tried to free her hand.

Cathy's eyes opened.

'I did tell you I wasn't crying because of Rob,' she murmured, and then she closed her eyes again.

Joanna went out of the main building and around the corner to the Maternity Block, and although she was already late, she walked slowly.

I was wrong about that, she admitted to herself, with some reluctance. I thought he'd hurt Cathy, and she was crying because of him. But he hadn't hurt her, then or any other time.

And then, painfully and inescapably, her thoughts followed through—if she had been wrong about that, could she not have been wrong about other things, to do with Rob Martin?

CHAPTER FOURTEEN

ONCE the thought was there, she couldn't escape it.

Somehow, from the moment she had met Rob Martin, she had been determined to see the worst in him. She had made up her mind that he was everything she disliked in a man—arrogant, sure of himself and sure of every girl he met.

And he isn't really that bad, Joanna admitted to herself, painfully, over the next few days. He works hard and he plays hard. He never makes promises, and he always remains friends with any girl he's known.

Except, of course, with me. I'm the odd one out, she reminded herself, I'm the one who wasn't prepared to fall at his feet, and I'm the one who wasn't prepared to give him a chance in any way.

Once, he had said to her that he thought they could have had fun together. She saw now that he was right—they could have had fun, if she hadn't made such a big deal out of having nothing to do with him.

But suddenly, like an abyss yawning before her, the thought of 'having fun' with Rob, of a short and merry episode in her life and his, was so infinitely disturbing that she couldn't let herself think about it.

All right, she told herself quickly, I've admitted to myself that Rob Martin isn't quite the big bad wolf I thought he was, and—and that will do quite nicely. I certainly don't plan to go overboard about him, because he's still far from being Mr Nice Guy!

Her time of night duty had finished, and she was very grateful for that, for the chance to get her metabolism back to knowing what it was doing, she said to Lynn.

'It's the upside-down feeling of everything that gets me,' she explained, and Lynn nodded sympathetically.

'It's bad enough now,' she agreed, 'but you'll find these couple of days before you start on District, you'll sleep almost solid, and then you'll feel human again.' She looked at the tiny but sparkling diamond on her left hand. 'I'm thinking of looking for a clinic job, Jo, these nursing hours would be hell after we're married.'

'How soon are you planning to get married?' Joanna asked her.

'As soon as possible,' Lynn told her. 'Quiet wedding—Michael's family are all in Ireland, I shouldn't think any of them will manage to come, but we would like to go over and visit them next year—get that out of the way before we start having a family.'

Joanna crushed a tiny feeling of envy for the warmth and the certainty in her friend's voice.

'I thought you said doing midder was enough to put you off babies,' she reminded Lynn, smiling.

'Babies in general, sure,' Lynn agreed. 'But it's a different thing when you start thinking of your own baby. I can't wait to have a little boy who looks just like Michael!'

She took the nail varnish Joanna had been using to paint her toenails, and began to do her own.

'No regrets, about you and Colin?' she asked, her head bent.

'None at all,' Joanna told her, with complete certainty. 'I'm not just saying this, Lynn, but I did know that Colin and I weren't right together, even before I knew about Cathy.'

'I know you did,' Lynn replied, and now she looked up. 'You just wouldn't admit it to yourself or to anyone else! You can be pretty stubborn sometimes, Joanna Winter.'

'I know that,' Joanna agreed, a little sadly, thinking of how stubborn she had been about Rob Martin. 'How was Cathy when you saw her today?'

'Coming on, but slowly,' said Lynn, finished with the nail varnish. 'But that isn't surprising, she almost didn't make it. A friend of mine who works in the ICU told me they didn't expect her to last through that first day, when there was no response to the drugs. She's a lucky girl.'

'I saw Colin yesterday, when I went to see Cathy,' said Joanna. 'Now that her parents have gone, she's beginning to ask about getting out of hospital, so Colin wants her to spend some time with his family at Hermanus, because she won't be able to start work again for some time.'

She stood up, and looked admiringly at her own gleaming toenails, and at Lynn's.

'Why do we bother, do you think?' she said, and smiled. 'Is it a gesture of defiance, because we're not allowed to have our fingernails painted while we're on duty?'

'I'll tell you this much,' her friend returned. 'You're starting on District—you can do with all the brightening up you can get, even if no one else can see it!'

Being on District, attached to the Outside Obstetrical Unit where she and Rob had gone with the Flying Squad, meant long hard days—even longer and harder than anywhere else, she sometimes thought—combining visits to mothers who had returned home with their new babies, with work in the wards.

'These women haven't always come regularly for check-ups,' the Sister in charge explained to her. 'They can, and they should, but—well, we still sometimes get a woman turning up for the first time, well into the second stage of labour! You'll learn a lot here, Nurse Winter, I can promise you, and one of the things you'll learn is to think and act fast!'

And that, Joanna found, was very true. On her second day working in Labour Ward, she did three deliveries right after each other, with barely time to scrub up in between. Lynn had told her that when she was on District it sometimes happened that there wasn't even time for the midwife to put her gloves on before delivering, and Joanna could well believe that now.

After her first week, she went out with one of the Sisters to do house visits. The condition of mother and baby had to be checked and recorded, and any problems were referred to the hospital. Doing visits on a Sunday morning, in one of the districts near the unit, Joanna's nose wrinkled in appreciation of the delicious smells of curry coming from all around. One of the young Indian mothers, when Joanna had checked, recorded, and admired her little dark-eyed baby boy, shyly offered Joanna a taste of the curry simmering in the pot.

'Have some, you'll never taste curry like it,' Sister Areef, herself Indian, persuaded Joanna. And she was right, Joanna thought, as she tasted the distinctive flavour and thanked the young mother.

A little later, she was only too glad of the strengthening effects of the curry, when she went ahead of Sister Areef into a block of flats. The midwives always knocked, and then, if no one came to the door, opened it and went in, as often the new mother might be busy with her baby, and unable to come.

At the first door Joanna knocked, and when no one came she opened the door, calling out at the same time. But as the door began to open, suddenly a dog was there—a bull terrier, she realised later—barking, and slavering, and very, very hostile. Hastily, her heart thudding, Joanna shut the door, only just in time, and waited for Sister Areef, who was plump and comfortable, to join her at the door.

Breathlessly she explained what had happened.

'That's only Tiger,' the older woman told her, smiling.

'Only?' repeated Joanna, thinking of the slavering jaws.

'Mrs Kariem,' Sister Areef called in through the window. 'It's Sister—let us in, please!'

With some trepidation Joanna followed her into the house. The bull terrier, a changed animal now, sat affectionately at her feet as she examined the baby and made her notes.

'You don't need to worry about him, Sister,' his owner said, and Joanna, accustomed now to her sudden increase in position, for all the nurses were called Sister by the patients, felt brave enough to pat the dog's head. 'He'll know you next time.'

'Maybe he will,' Joanna said to Sister Areef as they went downstairs and on to their next visit, 'but I'll do just as you did, and call in the window first!'

A few days later she was working in Labour Ward, had just delivered a little girl, and was waiting for Sister's instruction to give an intramuscular injection to help to expel the placenta, which was a long time in coming, when the other student midwife, attending to the baby, mentioned that the baby was smaller than they had expected from Mrs Brown's last check-up.

Sister, preparing the injection, stopped. And Joanna thought later, with humility, that this was where years of experience made the world of difference in midwifery.

'Just a minute,' she said sharply. 'I want to examine her again.'

Joanna handed her a sterilised glove, and watched, puzzled by the older woman's reaction, during the examination.

'No injection,' she said briefly. 'Nurse Carter, stay with Mrs Barnes. Nurse Winter, come with me.'

Joanna followed her through to the tiny Duty Room, and watched as she lifted the telephone and began dialling.

'Undiagnosed twins,' she said to Joanna. And then—'Flying Squad. Hanover Park here—emergency. We have a patient here who has delivered one twin, the other is lying transverse. She delivered five minutes ago—yes, we'll have her completely ready for theatre, drip will be set up. You'll be quick?'

She put the phone down, and as Joanna followed her back to the ward she explained.

'There's no chance of a normal delivery, the second baby is lying transverse—I actually felt its hand. It will have to be a Caesar, and now that the first one is born, there's a danger of anoxia. What we're going to do is stop the contractions, now, and hold everything until the Flying Squad gets here, and takes her to hospital.'

The other lesson Joanna learned that day was when she saw Sister, before all the frantic activity started, take the time to explain to her patient what was happening, and what they were doing. Because if she hadn't, Joanna thought, as they fixed up the drip and made their patient ready for the trip to the hospital, and right into theatre, it would have been extremely alarming, to say the least.

She knew, from her own experience on the Flying Squad, just how quickly they responded to an emergency, but all the same it seemed so long until the ambulance drew up and a doctor and a nurse hurried out. Rob Martin, she saw, and even in the middle of her concern about their patient, there was a ridiculous uneven thudding around her heart. But there was no time to give house room to any thoughts like that, and the next few minutes were all activity, restrained but fairly frantic, as the Flying Squad team got their patient into the ambulance, the nurse positioned where she could keep a constant check on the drip. For a moment, remembering her own times with the Flying Squad, Joanna felt a stab of envy at the thought of this nurse being an ongoing part of the drama of this undiagnosed twin birth, while she was out of it now.

'We'll give you a ring and let you know,' said Rob,

suddenly and unexpectedly, 'as soon as we have any news.'

Just for a moment he smiled, right at her. Nothing personal, of course, Joanna reminded herself quickly—not that she wanted or needed anything personal from Rob Martin! He probably hadn't even noticed that it was her, she told herself.

But an hour later, when the phone rang, and she answered it, Rob said:

'Joanna?' And then, as if regretting that, 'Ah, Nurse Winter. Please tell Sister Areef that everything is fine. A tiny baby, and a little distressed when we got him out, but he's in an incubator and doing nicely. Thought you girls would like to know.'

He rang off then, before she could even thank him, but she went off to tell the rest of the staff, for the news had spread quickly around the small Unit, and everyone breathed a sigh of relief at the safe delivery of the second twin.

The remainder of Joanna's time on District went unbelievably quickly, and in no time at all, it seemed to her, she was back in the familiar surroundings of the hospital, reporting for duty. Now she was to be working with the patients who were brought in and hospitalised for a few weeks before the birth of their babies.

'Hypertension, diabetes, pulmonary tuberculosis, renal disease—these account for most of our patients at the moment. Here are the charts—I'd like you to familiarise yourself with them,' Sister Bryan said, on Joanna's first day.

Most of the patients, Joanna found, weren't

seriously ill, but had to be in hospital for constant observation.

'To make sure we behave ourselves, Nurse,' one young woman with diabetes said mischievously. 'Personally, with this my third baby, I'm only too glad to do what I'm told and come in here and rest!'

And, Joanna knew, to have her insulin level constantly checked, for if it fell abruptly, between the thirtieth and the thirty-seventh week, it could be a sign of impending or actual foetal death. She knew that young Marty Jones was well aware of this, for sometimes, behind her light chatter and her smile, Joanna would see a sudden shadow, and feel the need for reassurance.

During her first few days Rob, like the other doctors and registrars, was in and out of the ward fairly often, as these were the patients who needed constant medical attention. One day, when he had been in to check a newly-admitted patient, he followed Joanna to the Duty Room.

'I've spoken to Sister,' he said to her, when she looked up from the desk where she had started completing Helen Campbell's chart, 'but I wanted to have a word with you too. As you know from her chart, she's suffering from cardiac disease. She must have complete bed rest, and I want to be called if there's any deterioration in her condition at all.'

He looked at her consideringly.

'You're a good nurse,' he said unexpectedly, 'and I don't say that lightly. And above and beyond the professional skill I expect from you, such as a constant watch for anaemia, respiratory infection, atrial fibrillation or other arrhythmia, give her all the support you can.' His dark blue eyes were clouded. 'She should never had had this child,' he said, his voice low. 'If she'd come to us right at the start, we would of course have advised abortion, her health certainly warrants it. But—' he smiled, although his eyes were still shadowed, 'I've got to know Helen Campbell and her husband fairly well in these past months, and she is one stubborn lady. She wants to give her husband a son, and she's determined to do just that, even if—'

He stopped, then, not saying the words. And Joanna thought again, as she had so often before, that as well as being a good doctor, he was a—a caring, feeling doctor. Following on that, suddenly, was another thought—perhaps this was the real Rob Martin.

'I'll look after Mrs Campbell,' she said steadily.

'I know you will,' he replied. For a moment she thought he was going to say something more, but he turned away to look for Sister before he left.

With complete bed rest ordered, Helen Campbell needed a great deal of nursing, and Joanna felt that she got to know her patient well in a short time. Helen, only a few years older than Joanna herself, was quiet and uncomplaining—but there was more to her than that, Joanna decided. There was an inner core of strength, of resolve, that gave an unexpected extra quality to her sweetness.

'He's very active today,' she said to Joanna one afternoon, when Joanna was rubbing her back. 'Maybe he's going to be a rugby player like his daddy.'

'You always say he,' Joanna commented. 'Most women hedge their bets, and say he or she—or even it, which I hate!'

'It is a boy,' Helen said serenely. And then, with that deep-down steeliness, 'It has to be, Joanna. There—won't be any more, I know that, and David does want a son. And I want to give him one.'

Another day, she told Joanna of his family's opposition to their marriage, because of her health.

'David's father has a huge sugar plantation, north of Durbank,' she said. 'David is the third David Campbell of Glenalmond. Apparently the world might just come to an end if there wasn't a fourth David Campbell.' She patted her distended stomach. 'But there is—right here!'

Joanna knew well enough that it was a mistake to become personally involved in any way with your patients, but there was no way she could avoid becoming fond of Helen Campbell. And no way she could avoid being very distressed when she arrived on duty one day to find that during the night Helen had gone into acute heart failure. Rob Martin had been sent for immediately.

'He's been here all night,' Sister Bryan told her. 'He's cautious, but he thinks she'll make it.'

This time.

The words hadn't been said, but they were there, unspoken.

'Eveything possible is being done,' the Sister went on. 'She's had oxygen, we have her propped up, and on morphine and a diuretic. Pressure respiration, too, and mechanical suction. Dr Martin wants her apex beat recorded hourly, and the physiotherapist is going to come in and give her massage and exercise for her legs, to avoid venous thrombosis.'

She looked at her watch.

'I think Mr Campbell has gone now,' she said. 'Do that apex beat check now, please, Nurse Winter. And try not to look so anxious!'

With a conscious effort Joanna put a smile on her face before she went into Helen Campbell's room. And with the smile, a professional attitude, she reminded herself.

She was glad of that professional attitude.

Helen Campbell was propped up, to increase her vital capacity, and she was asleep. So deeply asleep that she barely stirred when Joanna recorded her apex beat, and checked the drip, and the ventilator, at the ready. And then, and only then, she looked across at Rob Martin, in the armchair near the window.

He was asleep, and he was exhausted. His dark lashes—much too long for a man, she found herself thinking, absurdly—lay on his cheeks, and his hair was untidy. He needed a shave. He doesn't look so good now, Joanna thought coolly, detachedly.

And then, as she stood looking at him, slowly, surely, that coolness and detachment seeped out of her.

I want to go to him, she thought painfully. I want to put my arms around him, and hold him close to me, and never let him go.

Afterwards, she wondered if she might have done just that, if he hadn't right at that moment opened his eyes.

'Joanna?' he said, his voice blurred with weariness.

And again, wonderingly:

'Joanna?'

CHAPTER FIFTEEN

SOMEHOW Joanna managed to recover, and managed to hide from Rob this sudden and devastating discovery of how she really felt about him.

'I'm sorry I woke you, Dr Martin,' she said, quietly, pleasantly—a perfect nurse-to-doctor voice, she told herself afterwards. 'I was checking on Mrs Campbell.'

He was awake now, the exhaustion hidden, and the unnerving and unexpected vulnerability gone. He held out his hand for the chart she had just filled in, and she handed it to him.

'Dr Martin? Joanna?'

Helen Campbell's voice was little more than a thread, but it was enough. Both Rob and Joanna swung round.

'Let me ask you first,' she said, and with an effort she smiled. Joanna's heart ached for the courage of this young woman. 'How am I?'

Rob smiled too. 'A heck of a lot better than you were a few hours ago,' he told her honestly. 'You gave us quite a fright, but everything's coming right.'

'My baby?' asked Helen, her voice unsteady.

'Your baby is fine,' Rob told her, with truth, for the foetal heartbeat was reassuringly steady. 'We sent your husband home, he looked worse than you did!'

'Poor David,' Helen said softly. 'Does he know I'm much better now?'

166

For a moment Rob's eyes met Joanna's, and she knew that he, too, was thinking that the word 'much' perhaps said more than it should have.

'He wouldn't leave here until he knew that,' he said. 'Nurse Winter, now that my patient is behaving better, I'll go, but there are a couple of things I'd better check with Sister. I'll be back later to see you, Helen.'

He and Joanna walked along the corridor together, and Rob didn't say anything until they reached the Duty Room and found it empty.

'I'll give Sister a ring,' he said. 'And of course I'll look in. And I want to be called if there's any deterioration in her condition.'

Joanna nodded.

'What are her chances, Dr Martin?' she asked steadily.

He didn't answer right away.

'Not too good, Joanna,' he said at last, with sadness. She thought that he hadn't realised he had said Joanna, instead of Nurse Winter. 'Her general condition has worsened, and her heart itself is in really bad shape now.'

'She's thirty-four weeks now,' said Joanna. 'Couldn't you do a Caesar now, even if the baby is small for term?'

He shook his head.

'She'd never stand up to it,' he said simply. 'We can't risk doing anything to bring labour on, in the condition she's in now. When she does go into labour—and I hope that will be within the next couple of weeks—we'll use the vacuum extractor or the low forceps, to minimise distress to the heart.' And then, the professional note gone, he said quietly, 'It's all we can do, Joanna.'

'She wants her baby so much,' Joanna sighed shakily.

'She'll have her baby,' said Rob. But the concern was still in his eyes.

Sister came back then, and Joanna left Helen Campbell's chart with her and with Rob, as they discussed the immediate treatment, and the absolute necessity to keep Helen Campbell sedated and calm.

It was a full and busy day in the ward, and Joanna was glad of that, glad to put off facing the realisation of her feelings for Rob. But eventually the day was over and it was time to go back home. The little flat seemed very quiet and lonely, with Cathy still in hospital, and Lynn already back and out with Michael. For a moment Joanna had a stab of intense longing for her home, for her mother and father and her noisy young brothers and the dogs.

Ridiculously, she felt one solitary tear running down her cheek, and she brushed it away impatiently and went to make herself a cup of coffee. Then, sitting on the couch drinking her coffee, with her shoes off and her feet up, too tired to get out of her uniform, too tired to run the bath she was longing for, there was no more putting off that moment when she had stood looking at Rob asleep, that moment when she had known that she loved him.

It wasn't just chemistry, it wasn't just a physical response; she loved this man deeply and completely, she knew that with complete certainty. And she knew, too, now that she was finally being honest with herself, that she had been fighting against this admission from the first time she met him. She had been so sure, so certain that she knew the kind of man he was—and so determined that she wasn't going to be another of the girls falling at his feet.

Now—now that it was too late, she could see, painfully, how wrong she had been about him. All right, he liked fun, and he enjoyed having fun with any pretty girl, but he never had been anything but honest with any of the girls he had known.

He had said to her once, lightly, that he had just been waiting for the right girl. Perhaps that was true, and perhaps, Joanna thought with sadness, it might have been me, if I hadn't been so determined to see him as the hospital Casanova and nothing more. I—didn't give him a chance, and I didn't give us a chance.

Us.

Bleakly she faced the certainty that there was no 'us' as far as she and Rob were concerned. If she had made up her mind about him, she had also, over the months she had known him, gone a long way towards making up Rob Martin's mind about her.

How does he see me? she wondered now, forcing herself to be honest. A good nurse—yes, he had said that. A girl who had kept Colin on a string, neither wanting him herself nor wanting to let him go. A girl who had tried to break up his friendship—and friendship, true and simple, it had been—with Cathy. A girl who hadn't let go of Colin, even after Cathy was ill. Yes, all these things would go into the picture Rob had of Joanna Winter.

And yet—and yet there had been moments, moments she hugged to herself now, as she remembered.

His lips on hers, warm and demanding, his arms holding her close to him. His voice, sleepy, saying her name. His eyes, meeting hers in a shared moment of closeness.

'No,' Joanna said aloud, fiercely.

Because it was no good, spreading out these precious moments and lingering over them. She had better be honest and clear-sighted about this. If she ever had had any chance at all with Rob Martin, she had thrown it away—not only once, but many times.

And of course, being Rob, he would have no problem finding someone to console him, if he should happen to need any consolation. And then, with a revival of spirit and of pride—And neither would I.

That, without being falsely modest, was very true, as she found out in the next few days. Somehow word had got around that she and Colin were no longer a pair, and she had more invitations than she had free time. She went out three nights in succession, once for a drink at the Pig and Whistle, then to a disco in a nightclub, and then to dinner and a show, with Larry Keet, who was tall and good-looking and confident, and headed for the top in gynaecology.

The night they were at the Pig, she thought she saw Rob at the far side of the crowded room, but it was only a glimpse, and the familiar fair head had gone within a few moments. She hadn't been able to see, either, who was with him.

Like the old song, one of her mother's favourites, she found herself humming—I wonder who's kissing him now?

And then, abruptly, stopping herself, because the last thing she wanted to think of was anyone else in

Rob's arms, anyone else kissing him now or at any other time.

Sometimes the violence of her own feelings shook her, and she began to realise, painfully and with difficulty, that perhaps this was what she had been afraid of, when she had spent so much time and energy resisting falling for him. Because she had known, deep down, that if once she let herself fall in love with him it would be different from anything she had ever known, it would be a flood of emotion she would have no control over. And she might as well have given in to it right then, for all the good her holding out had done her.

Each time she visited Cathy, she took care to stand outside the room for a moment, listening to make sure that Rob wouldn't be there, not sure, sometimes, whether it would hurt more to see him or not to see him. Out of the context of their work, of course, she meant, as she saw him almost daily on the ward, but that was a different thing. There never had been any problems between Rob Martin the doctor and Joanna Winter the nurse, they always had got on well together, worked well together, understood each other.

When Cathy left hospital to go and spend some time with Colin's parents, convalescing, she made Joanna promise to come to Hermanus on her first free weekend. Helen Campbell still wasn't at her due date, and in any case Joanna wouldn't be on duty that weekend. Colin had hoped to go for the weekend as well, but found that he couldn't get away, so Joanna drove all the way alone, in her little German car, trying hard all the time not to remember the other

Hermanus weekend. And wishing, more than once, that she hadn't promised Cathy she would come.

But she was very glad that she had, for Cathy was so pleased to see her, and so were Colin's parents. In the hospital, she and Cathy had had very few chances to talk with any degree of privacy, and Joanna found that Cathy welcomed this chance to clear the air as much as she did.

'I didn't know whether to believe you or not, when you kept saying it was all right,' Cathy confessed. 'I just couldn't think any girl could know Colin and not be in love with him.'

Joanna took a moment or two before she replied to this.

'Colin is one of the nicest men I know,' she said at last, slowly. 'And—yes, good-looking, good company, all these things. But as for being in love—there has to be a spark, Cathy, that goes beyond any of these things, and that spark just wasn't there. It wasn't there for Colin either, he just took a little longer to see it. We'd become a habit with each other, a pleasant habit, but a habit.'

'No spark,' Cathy murmured thoughtfully to herself. 'That's what Rob said.'

Joanna's heart lurched treacherously.

'Rob?' she echoed, surprised to find that her voice was fairly steady. 'What—else did he say?'

'Nothing much, really,' Cathy replied, abstractedly. 'That was before I knew that—that Colin loved me. Rob said he thought both you and Colin just needed time to realise that there wasn't enough—magic, I think he said—between the two of you.'

Spark—magic—call it what you will, Joanna thought bleakly. It was there all right between Rob and me, if only J hadn't been too blind to see it.

Determinedly, she took her thoughts away from Rob and asked Cathy if she and Colin had made any plans.

'Not really,' Cathy told her, colouring a little. 'Just—when I'm well enough, we'll go up and see my parents, and maybe we'll get engaged after that.'

They went for a short walk along the cliff path after that, with Colin's mother reminding Joanna anxiously not to let Cathy overtire herself. In the evening, they played Scrabble and went early to bed, and Joanna thought that she had enjoyed this quiet family evening much more than she had the three evenings she had gone out on dates.

She slept much longer than she had intended to the next morning, and came through to a kitchen bright with winter sunshine, and Cathy and Mrs Cameron sitting talking at the kitchen table.

'Scrambled egg all right for you, Joanna? Good, I'll do yours right now,' Mrs Cameron said comfortably. 'Then we'll clear up, just in case Rob does come.'

Joanna, her glass of fruit juice halfway to her mouth, found that she had frozen, as if she was playing Statues.

'Rob said he had a day off, and he just might look in,' Cathy explained. 'But there's nothing definite.'

Joanna ate her scrambled egg and her toast, and tried to still her whirling thoughts. Ridiculous even to hope, but—away from the hospital, away from Cape Town—Suddenly she was glad she had brought her new pink track suit with her, it was such a pretty colour, and the pants were a good sleek fit, much nicer than most track suits. And I washed my hair yesterday too, she thought thankfully.

'You're miles away, Joanna,' Cathy said. 'Come back!'

'Still half asleep,' Joanna apologised, completely untruthfully.

She helped to clear up breakfast, then went to her room to change, and brush her hair.

'You do look nice, Joanna,' said Cathy. 'I suppose I've missed out on most of the new winter things.'

'They're going fast,' Joanna agreed. She hoped that Cathy wouldn't suggest a walk, for she wanted to be right here, just in case—

'Maybe we'll go for a walk in the afternoon,' Cathy suggested. 'Let's just sit in the garden, and take advantage of a winter's day when we can do that. Tell me all about Lynn and Michael, now.'

The two girls sat in the pleasant garden looking out to sea, and talked, and Joanna was glad that Cathy didn't seem to be her usual perceptive self, and didn't see that Joanna's thoughts weren't always too closely on their conversation.

It was just after Mr and Mrs Cameron had left for church that a car drew up.

'That must be Rob,' Cathy said eagerly, rising from her deckchair.

Joanna stood up too, just as Rob came round the corner.

'Hi, Cathy,' he called cheerfully, shading his eyes against the sun. 'How's my best girl?' And then, stopping, 'Oh—Joanna, I didn't expect—I didn't see your car—'

Rob, somewhat at a loss. It shook her. Absurdly, she heard herself explaining that her car was at the back.

'I'm so glad you came, Rob,' said Cathy, slipping her arm through his.

He looked down at her and smiled, and then, for just one moment, his eyes met Joanna's.

'I brought someone with me,' he told Cathy. 'Thought you might enjoy some company.' He turned, then. 'Hurry up, Megan,' he said impatiently.

The girl was tall and blonde, blue eyes friendly in a suntanned face.

'Hi, Cathy,' she said easily. 'Aren't you Sarah Eaton's cousin? She and I trained together at Jo'burg Gen.'

Pleasantly, politely, Rob introduced Joanna to her. Some of Joanna's set had gone to Johannesburg General when they qualified, and it turned out that Megan knew most of them. They talked, the three girls, about the other nurses they knew, and compared aspects of their training, for there was always a friendly rivalry between the training hospitals. Joanna thought afterwards, objectively, that she had contributed as much talk and as much laughter as any of the three of them.

Rob and Megan wouldn't stay for lunch, explaining that they had brought a picnic with them. They had a cup of coffee, and some of Mrs Cameron's short-bread, then they left.

Just as Rob closed the door for Megan, he turned to Joanna.

'I phoned to check on Helen Campbell,' he told her quietly. 'Everything is fine, no sign of her going into labour.' He kissed Cathy's cheek lightly, easily. 'Look after yourself, Cathy. See you!'

'Nice girl, Megan,' Cathy commented as Rob's car turned the corner and disappeared from sight.

'Yes—very,' agreed Joanna, meaning it. Oh yes, she thought, a very nice girl, she and Rob will have fun. I wonder where they'll go for their picnic? I wonder if he'll take her to the little beach at de Kelders, the little beach where we went, he and I, when we came out of the cave.

'Joanna—' Cathy began uncertainly, but to Joanna's great relief Colin's parents came home at that moment, and soon after that Colin phoned, then it was lunchtime, and when they went for a walk on the cliffs afterwards, Mr and Mrs Cameron came as well. They had tea after that, then it was time for Joanna to leave for the drive back to Cape Town.

'It's been so nice seeing you, Joanna,' Cathy said, hugging her. 'I wish—'

Joanna looked at her friend.

'What do you wish, Cathy?' she asked, in spite of herself, but Cathy only coloured, and changed the subject.

'Let me know what happens with your special patient, will you, Joanna?' she asked, and Joanna promised that she would.

Next morning, when Joanna went on duty, she went in to see Helen as soon as she could, and the young mother-to-be's eyes lit up.

'I'm so glad you're on duty again, Joanna,' she said. 'Surely it won't be long now.'

But it was four days later before Helen went into labour. Joanna had been off the afternoon before, and she had phoned to find out, because Helen had had vague pains just before she left.

'Mrs Campbell says she's waiting for you to be on duty tomorrow,' her friend Tracey reported when Joanna called.

And it was soon after Joanna went on duty the next day that Helen Campbell went into the first stage of labour. Rob was informed right away, and he put her on continuous epidural analgesia, and set up a slow pump to control her intravenous fluid intake.

'I'm going to be in and out all the time,' he reassured his patient, 'and Nurse Winter will be with you.' He patted Helen's hand. 'I've told Sister to call your husband too. You're doing fine.'

But in the corridor, he looked down at Joanna, and his eyes were shadowed.

'We can't risk causing that heart any distress at all, she just can't take it,' he said quietly. 'I want her pulse and respirations recorded every fifteen minutes, and any increased breathlessness or cyanosis, you send for me stat.'

Surprisingly, for a first baby, Helen went into the second stage only five hours later, and there had been no need to send for Rob, as her condition had remained stable. He had come in three times, though, and as Joanna knew without him telling her, it was the second stage that would be dangerous.

As so often happened, once she went into second stage labour, things began to move quickly. Rob was there, scrubbed up, his mask on, explaining to Helen that he was going to do an episiotomy and a low forceps delivery. The cardiac specialist who had been treating Helen arrived too, and she was given oxygen continuously. David Campbell, masked too, stood quietly in a corner of the theatre, and it was only occasionally, in the middle of all the activity, that Joanna, handing an instrument to Rob, or taking a swab from him, saw the anxiety in Helen's husband's eyes, and tried, above her own mask, to give him a brief smile.

Carefully Rob finished his incision and began to ease the baby out. Joanna saw a look exchanged between Rob and the cardiac specialist, and gathered that so far, Helen's condition hadn't deteriorated.

'Here we go,' Rob muttered, and not for the first time Joanna admired the skill of a forceps delivery. 'Ready, Nurse?'

And then, with a swiftness that always surprised her, he delivered the baby completely, and Helen's little boy was in Joanna's arms.

'You've got your son, Helen,' Rob said jubilantly. 'Bring him here, Nurse. Give him to her, just as he is.'

Bonding, right at birth, so important, the student midwives had been taught. It was a moment that never failed to move Joanna, but she thought that she had never been as touched as she was right now, when Helen Campbell held her newly-born son in her arms, and her husband came over and kissed her, as they listened to their baby's first cry.

'All right, we're going to clean him up now, Helen, and make you comfortable,' Rob told her.

Joanna took the baby over to the prepared crib, and it was just after she had wrapped him up warmly that she heard the sudden, deep moment of silence behind her, then the frenzied activity, the cardiac specialist's swift instructions, Rob's reply, Sister's voice.

And then silence. But a different silence, now.

She turned round, knowing, but not wanting to admit it.

'She's gone, David,' Rob told the young husband wearily.

'She can't be,' David Campbell said unsteadily. 'She came through the actual delivery—'

Joanna heard the cardiac specialist explain, then, that collapse often occurred when the retracted uterus returned blood to the general circulation, and temporarily overloaded the heart. She heard Rob tell David Campbell that his baby son was fine.

She herself went on with what had to be done for the baby, her hands doing the familiar professional things, her mind shut off. She even, she recalled later, helped to tidy the theatre, efficiently, carefully.

And then suddenly Sister was there, telling her kindly that she was to go off duty now, she wasn't needed for anything else. Joanna thanked her politely and went to collect her cloak. She had walked to work that morning, because her car wouldn't start, and when she went outside she found it was raining, so she wrapped her cloak more tightly around her and began to walk home.

She had just turned the corner when Rob caught up with her. He hadn't stopped for a coat, and his white coat was wet.

'I'm sorry, Joanna,' he said simply. 'I'm sorry we couldn't save her.'

She looked at him, and now she saw her own distress, surfacing through the numbness, mirrored in his eyes. Not knowing she was going to do it, she began to cry, her tears mingling with the rain on her face.

He put his arms around her.

'Cry all you want to, my love,' he said unevenly.

And it was only much later, when she had wept for Helen Campbell, when her tears were over, that Joanna remembered what he had said.

CHAPTER SIXTEEN

'I'LL take you home, Joanna,' Rob said at last.

'Shouldn't you be with David Campbell?' she asked him.

He shook his head. 'His brother has taken him home. I asked him to be there, in case David needed him.'

He buttoned her cloak, his fingers cold and wet with rain against her chin, and they walked the rest of the way back to the flat without speaking. Joanna unlocked the door and they went in.

'I'll make coffee—get changed into something warm and dry,' Rob told her.

'You're wet too,' Joanna pointed out, but he shrugged.

'If you give me a towel, I'll rub my hair dry,' he said.

She went through to her room and brought a towel for him, and the biggest sweater she had. Then she went back and did as he had told her, changed, and rubbed her hair until it was almost dry. When she went back to the kitchen, he was wearing her sweater, and his thick fair hair was carelessly rubbed dry. For a moment, seeing him, she almost smiled, and then she remembered.

'Have some coffee, and tell me where I can find a heater,' he said brusquely, and she was glad of his brusqueness, for if he had been kind, right at that moment when her mind was filled with thoughts of

Helen dying, she would have wept again. And I can't go on crying, she told herself.

'The heater's in that corner,' she told him, 'behind the carpet cleaner.'

She lifted it out and switched it on, then sat down beside him at the kitchen table and drank the hot sweet coffee, realising only then just how cold she was.

'The really incredible thing,' he said at last, slowly, 'is that she managed to hold on to life as long as she did. The heart man—Cliff Bayne—told me months ago that whether or not Helen had been pregnant, she couldn't have lived much longer. There was no surgery that could have corrected the massive heart defects she had.'

Joanna's hands were round the hot mug of coffee, and slowly she was beginning to feel warm again.

'Did she know that?' she asked Rob steadily.

He nodded.

'They both knew it,' he said soberly. 'Joanna, her pregnancy didn't shorten her life by more than a few months, and you know how much she wanted to give David a son. Will you ever forget the way she looked, when she held the baby, when she knew that she'd done what she wanted? It was her one perfect moment, and I don't think she would have wanted these extra few months, at the price of not giving David the son they both wanted.'

Across the kitchen table she looked at him, and didn't know that she was crying again until he leaned over and gently wiped the tears from her cheeks.

'If only she could have had her son *and* her life,' she said shakily.

He came round, then, and held her while she wept for the young woman she had grown so fond of in these weeks of waiting, for the young man who had loved her, and for the child who would grow up and never know his mother.

And when her tears were over Rob went on just holding her, saying nothing, doing nothing, just being there, and giving her comfort by being there.

'Joanna, I'm going back to the hospital,' he said at last, and she nodded, accepting this. She went with him to the door, carrying his white coat, still wet from the rain.

'What will you do?' she asked him, a little unevenly. 'Your coat's still wet.'

'I'll borrow one,' he said. 'I'll keep your sweater, though.'

He looked down at her, and she remembered, then, what he had said to her as they stood in the rain. My love, he had said. Slow, warm colour suffused her cheeks.

'Tomorrow,' he said to her steadily. 'You finish your weeping for Helen, and I'll see you tomorrow. You're off, aren't you? I'll be off in the afternoon—I'll pick you up at two.'

She did weep more for Helen that day, and that night, but she kept reminding herself of what Rob had said, that Helen couldn't have lived much longer. He was right, she thought painfully. Helen did have her one perfect moment, and she was completely happy, when she held her baby. That is something. And as for David—if Helen hadn't somehow gone ahead and managed to have the baby, he would have been left with nothing but memories. Now he has his son, his and Helen's son.'

By morning, although she had wept many more tears, she had come to terms with Helen's death and had reached some sort of acceptance. She had told Lynn, and she had written to tell Cathy, and she knew that both her friends understood, and had had similar feelings and experiences in their nursing. Lynn didn't say much, and Joanna was grateful for that.

She was ready when Rob came for her. When she opened the door he stood for a long time, looking down at her. Then, as if he felt happier, he nodded.

'Bring a thick sweater and a raincoat,' he told her. 'Your jeans and these shoes will do fine.'

Once she would have argued with him, just because she didn't want to agree. Right now, she didn't need to argue.

'Where are we going?' she asked him in the car.

'Over the Nek to Camp's Bay,' he told her. 'It probably isn't raining there.'

It wasn't, although the sky above the sea was still grey and stormy, as they dropped down the steep road. When the car drew up outside Rob's cottage, Joanna could hear Rufus inside, barking in welcome.

'He knows it's my car,' Rob told her. 'Different bark for strangers.' He unlocked the door. 'And I told him I was bringing you today,' he added, and just for a moment his eyes held hers with an intimacy as close as if he had held her. Then the big dog was there, his plumed tail waving in greeting.

'He remembers me!' Joanna exclaimed with pleasure, glad to bend down to the dog.

'Of course he does,' Rob agreed. 'Joanna, I'm

going to light the fire now, then we'll have a brisk walk on the beach before the rain comes. Is that all right with you? The fire will be going well by the time we get back.'

She watched him light the fire, and had a sudden certainty that there would be so many times, in the years to come, when she would see him doing just this, when they would stand together and watch the flames, slow at first and then warm and glowing.

'Let's have that walk,' said Rob, when the fire had settled. 'Come on, Rufus—walk!'

It was cold, and the rain wasn't far away, and the beach was deserted. He took Joanna's hand and held it, with his, in the pocket of his warm jacket. The big dog ran ahead of them, easily, gracefully.

They had just turned when the rain did start.

'Run,' Rob told her, and they ran, hand in hand, reaching the cottage just as the drops became heavier. They went inside, with Rufus shaking himself vigorously, and took their coats off.

'Tea and toast,' Rob said firmly, and made her sit at the fire and start making toast, while he brought tea through.

'No, you have to turn it to get it done evenly,' he explained, taking the toasting fork from her. 'Like this.'

'I didn't know you were so domesticated,' Joanna said.

His hand covered hers on the toasting fork.

'There's a lot you don't know about me,' he told her, his voice low.

She looked at him, as they knelt together in front of the fire.

'Is it wrong, Rob, for us to be happy, when just yesterday Helen died?' she asked him.

'No,' he replied, his voice steady. 'No, it isn't wrong. We have to accept death, in the work we do, but we have to accept life too. Life is Helen's little son, and life is us, you and me.'

She could say it now, because there was no room for pride, no room for anything but honesty—and there never again would be, she knew.

'Rob, yesterday you said—you called me your love.'

He put the toasting fork down and took both her hands in his.

'You are my love—you always have been,' he told her.

He kissed her then, gently at first, and then far from gently, his lips demanding and possessive on hers, his arms holding her as close as she had longed to be to him.

Later—much later—they finished making the toast, and Joanna made fresh tea, because the teapot was almost cold. Then they sat in front of the fire, very close.

'That girl—Megan?' she began.

'That doctor you were at the Pig with,' Rob returned, and smiled.

'I thought you were so arrogant, so sure every girl would fall for you,' she told him.

His arm tightened around her.

'And I thought you were just another girl to have fun with. A bit more of a challenge, maybe, and I thought I'd rather enjoy the challenge. I didn't realise, then, that I was going to fall in love with you,' he said, his lips against her hair.

'I went on fighting it for so long,' Joanna told him. 'I told myself it was just chemistry, purely physical, it meant nothing at all.'

He tilted her chin and kissed her again.

'Not too much wrong with the chemistry, though,' he murmured. 'Or do you still distrust chemistry?'

She moved closer to him. 'No, I don't mind it at all,' she told him, with complete honesty. 'But we've got so much more than—chemistry, haven't we?'

For now, in this small cottage, with the sea pounding outside, and the rain on the roof, and the fire in front of them, she knew that the two parts of this man had come together. The caring and conscientious doctor she had admired and worked with, and the good-looking and confident man who had stirred her senses so disturbingly—Rob, her love.

'Lots of weddings,' remarked Rob after a while, lazily. 'Michael and Lynn, Colin and Cathy, and us.'

'Wedding?' Joanna repeated, for the first time able to tease him. 'You haven't said anything about a wedding, Dr Martin.'

There was only the firelight, and she couldn't see him, but she could hear the smile in his voice.

'You mean you don't really care whether I make an honest woman of you or not?' he asked her. 'In that case, I'll risk it, with Rufus here as a witness. Joanna, will you marry me?'

Joanna turned round to face him.

'Yes, sir,' she told him, positively and happily, 'I certainly will. When?'

'Soon,' he said. 'Very, very soon.' And then, laughter in his voice, 'Actually, you'd better finish your exams first, you'll be much more use as a doctor's wife, with your midder qualification behind you.'

An apologetic bark from Rufus reminded Rob that this was the dog's supper time, and Joanna went with him to the small kitchen while he fed Rufus.

'Do you realise I don't know the first thing about your family?' he said to her. 'I want to meet them, and soon, but tell me about them.'

Joanna sat at the kitchen table and told him about her father, and the farm, and her mother, who had been a nurse too, and who still looked after the farm labourers and their wives and families. About her two young brothers, Tim and Steve, both still at school.

'And the dogs,' she said. 'Or maybe I should tell Rufus about the dogs.' She looked up at him. 'Tell me about your family, Rob,' she said softly.

'Just my mother and father,' he replied. 'You'll like them, Joanna, and they'll like you. My father is a doctor too, and my mother teaches disabled children. You—would have liked Laura.'

Joanna glanced through the open door at the photograph on the piano.

'Is Cathy really like her?' she asked him quietly.

'Yes, she is,' said Rob, after a moment. 'There's a superficial resemblance, but she's like Laura in her ways, somehow. Quiet, gentle, thoughtful. You see why I really do look on her as a sister.'

Joanna nodded. 'I see that,' she replied. 'And I'm so sorry, Rob, that I didn't believe you when you said that. Well, since I don't have a sister either, Cathy will have to be a sister for both of us!'

She looked at the clock.

'I'd no idea it was so late!' she exclaimed, taken

aback. 'Lynn will be wondering where on earth I am—I left her a note to say I was going out with you, so she'll be even more surprised that I'm so late.'

Rob shook his head.

'I wouldn't be too sure,' he told her. 'I think Lynn has a pretty good idea of how I feel about you, and maybe she has some idea that something like this just might happen, if you gave us half a chance.'

'I'm glad I did,' Joanna told him. 'Give us half a chance, I mean. Rob, listen—the rain has stopped.'

They went to the door and opened it. The rain had stopped, and the wind had blown the clouds away. High in the sky, the moon and the stars were clear.

'Are you working tomorrow, love?' asked Rob, and Joanna nodded. Tomorrow, she thought soberly, wouldn't be too easy, going back to the hospital, and seeing Helen Campbell's baby son in his crib in the nursery. But Rob was right; dying was part of the work they did, but so was living.

'Joanna,' he said, and when she turned to him he kissed her, a long, slow kiss.

'Maybe I'd better take you home,' he murmured at last, not quite steadily.

'Maybe you'd better,' she agreed.

She looked up at the clear sky. 'Tomorrow is going to be a nice day,' she told him.

Tomorrow, she thought—and all the tomorrows we'll have, together.

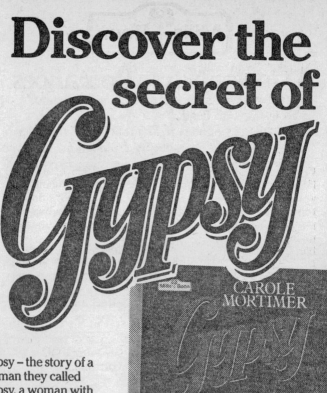

Mills & Boon

4 Doctor Nurse Romances
FREE

Coping with the daily tragedies and ordeals of a busy hospital, and sharing the satisfaction of a difficult job well done, people find themselves unexpectedly drawn together. Mills & Boon Doctor Nurse Romances capture perfectly the excitement, the intrigue and the emotions of modern medicine, that so often lead to overwhelming and blissful love. By becoming a regular reader of Mills & Boon Doctor Nurse Romances you can enjoy SIX superb new titles every two months plus a whole range of special benefits: your very own personal membership card, a free newsletter packed with recipes, competitions, bargain book offers, plus big cash savings.

AND an Introductory FREE GIFT for YOU.
Turn over the page for details.

Fill in and send this coupon back today
and we'll send you
4 Introductory
Doctor Nurse Romances yours to keep
FREE
At the same time we will reserve a
subscription to Mills & Boon
Doctor Nurse Romances for you. Every
two months you will receive the latest
6 new titles, delivered direct to your door.
You don't pay extra for delivery. Postage and
packing is always completely Free.
There is no obligation or commitment –
you receive books only for
as long as you want to.

It's easy! Fill in the coupon below and return it to
**MILLS & BOON READER SERVICE, FREEPOST, P.O. BOX 236,
CROYDON, SURREY CR9 9EL.**

Please note: **READERS IN SOUTH AFRICA write to**
Mills & Boon Ltd., Postbag X3010,
Randburg 2125, S. Africa.

— — — — — — — — — — — — — — — — — —

FREE BOOKS CERTIFICATE
**To: Mills & Boon Reader Service, FREEPOST, P.O. Box 236,
Croydon, Surrey CR9 9EL.**

Please send me, free and without obligation, four Dr. Nurse Romances, and reserve a Reader
Service Subscription for me. If I decide to subscribe I shall receive, following my free parcel
books, six new Dr. Nurse Romances every two months for £6.00 , post and packing free. If I
decide not to subscribe, I shall write to you within 10 days. The free books are mine to keep in
any case. I understand that I may cancel my subscription at any time simply by writing to you. I
am over 18 years of age.
Please write in BLOCK CAPITALS.

Name _____

Address _____

_____

_____ Postcode _____

SEND NO MONEY — TAKE NO RISKS

EP